GATEWAY

GATEWAY

LEE ROBINSON

HOUGHTON MIFFLIN COMPANY

BOSTON 1996

For information about this and other Houghton Mifflin
trade and reference books and multimedia products,
visit The Bookstore at Houghton Mifflin on the World
Wide Web at http://www.hmco.com/trade/.

Manufactured in the United States of America
Book design by Celia Chetham
The text of this book is set in 12 pt. Fairfield Medium
BP   10 9 8 7 6 5 4 3 2 1

Library of Congress Cataloging-in-Publication Data

Robinson, Lee.
Gateway / Lee Robinson.
p.   cm.
Summary: As her parents proceed with a divorce and
a custody battle over her, thirteen-year-old Margaret views
their activities with humor and good sense.
ISBN 0-395-72772-3
[1. Divorce — Fiction.]   I. Title
PZ7.R5667Gat   1996   95-17064
  [Fic] — dc20   CIP   AC

For my mother

ONE

I spent all Saturday morning, when I should have been sleeping, taking Harvey's stupid test.

I answered *Yes* to all of the following:

— I sometimes dream I am royalty.
— I often wish I were better looking.
— My parents sometimes ignore me.

I answered *No* to these:

— I am less intelligent than most of my friends.
— I think money can bring happiness.
— Most of my friends think of me as shy.

When I finished with the test, I told Harvey she should forget it.

"It doesn't get to the real problem," I said.

She looked interested. "Which problem?"

"The dream I keep having about being chased by giant red lizards down the streets of New York City until I fall into a manhole and die."

Harvey squinted her eyes. "Have you ever been to New York City?"

"Oh, lots of times" (which was close to the truth).

She asked me to tell her about New York, what I like and what I don't like.

I like the cabbies, the crazy traffic, the smoky smell of sausages and chestnuts cooking on the street corners. I don't like the pushy commuters, the slimy subway stairs, the way people waiting in lines won't look at you but stare out into space as if they have something really important to think about, which they probably don't.

I like Broadway shows, sitting so high up in the theater you might as well be hanging on to the side of a cliff. I like the orchestra tuning up. I don't like museums, except for the shops and the armor exhibit at the Metropolitan.

I like the lobby at the St. Moritz and feeling foreign because nobody around is speaking English. I do *not* like cheap little models of the Empire State Building. I do like pressing my nose against the glass at Windows on the World and watching my mother get nauseated.

I like the Christmas show at Radio City Music Hall because it has people ice skating right in front of you on a stage that rises out of nowhere.

I hate hot hotel rooms with windows that won't open. I like the ones with really big bathrooms and lots of miniature bottles of shampoo and hand lotion and silly things like lint removers and shower caps. I *really* like room service, although the last time we were in New York, my father told me I had to quit ordering shrimp cocktail and cherry Coke in the middle of the afternoon.

All of this is well and good, but Harvey wants more facts.

My favorite color: Black, if it is one. (This is not true, but I hope it will make me sound more interesting.) My favorite food: Rice and gravy. My biggest worry: I will grow up before I figure out what I want to do with my life. The grossest thing I can think of: Kissing my pimply math teacher.

Harvey wants to know about where I live.

My house is old and big. Historic. It used to be sort of funky before Mollie got hold of it and turned it into a showplace. Our house has been in magazines, even my bedroom.

I live downtown. I like being close to everything. Hal, my father, says we live in a dream world. Charleston is a dream world, he says. There's no

3

other city on earth like this. It moves in slow motion, it's so lovely and old. Everything is pastel and moving in slow motion like a dream. Hal likes that.

Wake up, Mollie says, stop dreaming. Mollie is my mother.

TWO

Hal and Mollie are getting a divorce. Harvey says I need to say this at least once a day: *Hal and Mollie are getting a divorce.* Then maybe I will convince myself this is really happening.

Harvey is my therapist. I see her once a week. Half the time I think she is full of it. She is always digging and digging. Lots of questions about how I feel. She makes me talk into this tape machine every day. The last thing I want to do is talk about how I feel. I feel lousy.

Harvey is not *totally* full of it. I really do think she is trying to help. She just doesn't know much about kids. Maybe that's because she's never had any. Maybe it's because most of the kids she sees are nuts, and she's not used to normal ones.

At least I used to be normal. Now I'm not so sure. Hal and Mollie are getting a divorce from each other, and I'm getting a divorce from both of them. At least I'd like to. They are bugging me, big time. They've hired Harvey to talk to me because they don't want to.

Not that I blame them. I've been a pain lately. I pout a lot. I let my snake out of its cage on purpose so *I* could have a crisis that had nothing to do with their divorce.

It worked for an afternoon. They were highly motivated to find Bal (a boa) before the housekeeper came. Hal came over to help look for the snake, even though it wasn't his day to visit. My parents got down on their hands and knees and crawled all over the house together looking. It was sweet, but it didn't get them back together.

Hal found Bal under Mollie's bed. He also found some other man's slippers. That made him really mad, and he went around yelling for a while. So *my* crisis got all messed up. He walked out of the house with great big heavy steps — marched out, really — and yelled, "You'll hear from my lawyer," before he slammed the door. Mollie cried for hours. She said the slippers were irrelevant.

That just goes to show how messed up her

thinking is. If I were a husband coming back to my house and I found some other man's slippers under my former bed, I'd be mad. Mollie just doesn't get it sometimes.

THREE

If I could, I would convene an emergency meeting of the Blue Hydrangea Society. I need my friends now. I need us all *together*. Edward and Evelyn are still around, and Tim may come back to Charleston this summer, but the Blue Hydrangea — all of us together — has fallen apart.

If I could snap my fingers and make us the way we used to be, we would ride our bikes over to the ruins of the old rice mill, behind the grocery store, where the one wall that's left rises up, right out of the past like a ghost, above the warehouses and the criss-crossed train tracks. You can see right through the windows to the harbor. It's like a house with no real insides. It was a good place to hold a secret meeting:

it was wide open, but nobody ever thought to look behind the wall.

Evelyn would be in charge of the meeting, even though I was the one who asked for it, because Evelyn was always in charge of everything. She would keep the minutes in her blue notebook, recording our discussions in her boring perfect handwriting with the little circles that dot the *i*'s and the fat loops underneath the *p*'s and *y*'s. Tim would bring something weird to eat, like mulberries off the tree next to his apartment, and Edward would bring his paperback Edgar Allan Poe in case we needed inspiration.

Evelyn would spread out the wall hanging her aunt brought back from Indonesia, which her mother decided was too strange to actually hang in their house, and we would all sit cross-legged on it, facing each other. We liked sitting on top of the tangle of little monsters from almost exactly the other side of the world. We were determined to be wild and strange like them, beastly if necessary, and mystical.

Evelyn would ask Edward to read the minutes of the last meeting. He would read slowly, as though he was in church and what he was reading was going to change the world.

He would read the story of how we got arrested at St. Luke's Hospital when we tried to visit Mr. Murgrave. He'd stumble over the words "St. Luke's Hospital" because Edward always seems to have too much spit in his mouth or something, and when he has to say a word with too many s's in it, he gets nervous and tries to talk with his mouth almost closed.

I need the Blue Hydrangea Society now, because I am not sure of anything anymore. It was a strange club, such an uncool thing to belong to. But it was so weird it made me feel normal — and maybe that's why I miss it so much now.

Evelyn and I were the original members. That was in the fifth grade. Mollie and Evelyn's mother played tennis together, and so we had the same babysitter on Wednesday afternoons, a college student who went to sleep the minute our parents walked out the door. She was blonde and beautiful, but she was always sleepy, and we took advantage of it. We went through her pocketbook: it was a treasure trove containing everything you needed to be a real adult — blue eye shadow, credit cards, and an address book with lots of markings. What did the little stars mean beside "Henry Harris"? And what about the exclamation points on either side of "Winston Magillis"?

Evelyn Hanahan and I were not a natural duo.

We had nothing in common. Evelyn was slick and smart, cool, like lime sherbet. I was more like ordinary ice cream, vanilla or something. But we were together every Wednesday afternoon for a year with a babysitter who slept all the time, so we had to make the best of it. We decided we needed to form a club.

The Blue Hydrangea Society, we called it, just because it sounded good. We had started looking for inspiration in Evelyn's mother's cookbooks, but nothing sounded right. "Tapioca" was a possibility, but when we read about the ingredients we decided against it. Then we moved on to the books on gardening, and when we came to "Hydrangea" we knew we had something. We said it over and over again. It was so foreign-sounding, we thought. But it was also full of importance, as if it had been around a long time, maybe Greek or Latin or something. We looked up the picture — a big cluster of small blue flowers, and we found some in Mollie's flower bed.

Now that we had a name for the club, it had to have a purpose. We considered collecting canned goods for the homeless, picking up litter on the beach, and selling candy bars for charity. But grownups were already doing all those things, and even though they were worthwhile, they seemed, well, kind of ordinary.

We decided what the world needed was more

inspiration, the kind of feeling you get when you read a great poem, or when you open a long letter from an old friend. I have to give Evelyn credit for the idea, though looking back on it, it seems odd that Evelyn, who was so cool about everything she did, would come up with such an uncool, old-fashioned idea.

We left our first message on Mrs. Mandelbaum's front porch. Mr. Mandelbaum had just died. The Mandelbaums had lived across the street forever, and I had watched Mr. Mandelbaum get older and older, his cane waving in front of him like a long un-steady finger. He got so old and feeble I thought he might just evaporate into thin air, which is what he did one day. He died without making a mess, and Mrs. Mandelbaum had already planned his funeral. So when she had buried him and given his clothes away to the Salvation Army she was not expecting to break down and boo-hoo, but that's what she did, right out there on the curb while I was waiting for carpool.

That night Evelyn stayed over. We had just come up with a name and a mission for our club, and here was the perfect opportunity to try it out.

She wrote the note, in round, neat letters: "We will miss Mr. M and we are thinking of you." It seemed the right kind of thing to say to

Mrs. Mandelbaum. She was a quiet, dignified old lady who wouldn't want anything too sentimental. We sneaked out of the upstairs porch door and down the outside stairs, into my backyard, where the blue hydrangea was blossoming in the moonlight. We picked one, and left it on Mrs. Mandelbaum's front porch where she would be sure to see it, next to the note we tucked halfway under the doormat so it wouldn't get blown away.

We meant to get up early enough to see Mrs. Mandelbaum come out to pick up her morning paper, to watch her face as she saw the flower and found the note, but we stayed up too late painting our fingernails and plucking our eyebrows. When we woke up the next morning it was after ten, and by then the flower and the note were gone.

That was the Society's first visit, but there were many others. We visited people in trouble and left our messages, not always with blue hydrangeas but with whatever we could steal out of neighborhood gardens, whatever happened to be blooming at the time.

FOUR

Harvey wants me to talk about how the trouble started.

It started when Mollie decided to have a life of her own. We were all sitting at the breakfast table. She put down the newspaper, took a sip of coffee, and said, as if it was nothing, "I want a life of my own." Just like that. No big deal, right?

I mean, here is this forty-something woman who drives her own car to her own office every day, runs her own business, has her own housekeeper who cleans her house, which might as well be her own because she's the only one who has any say-so about what happens in it. And this woman wants a life of her *own*?

Anyway, to get back to the story. Hal put down his

part of the newspaper, too. (He always has to take the B section, which has nothing in it but the crime report and the church news, and waits for Mollie to finish the first section, which takes forever.) He stared at her. He breathed the sort of deep breath that comes before a big decision. And then he made a major mistake.

"Mollie," he said, "I don't think you'd be satisfied if you had a whole damn planet all to yourself." He got up from the table, brushed the toast crumbs off his trousers, and left for work. He never even raised his voice.

You might wonder why this turned out to be the beginning of the end. And to understand that you have to go a long way back. Before me, even.

That was when they were just married and really in love. They were living on nothing and going to graduate school. Mollie was into art history and Hal was studying problem children — something like learning disabilities, I think. He wanted to teach teachers how to teach.

Then Mollie changed the plan.

Mollie decided it was okay to want money, it was okay to talk about wanting money, and that she was going to find a way to make money and make Hal make money, too.

So she decided Hal needed to quit wasting time

learning about problem children, which is a fine thing to do with your life, but after all, let's get practical (I can just hear her saying it), you're never going to make any money that way.

Mollie decided Hal needed to go to law school. And before he knew it, he thought it was a fine idea.

And Mollie dumped her dissertation and went into design. Not *interior* design. She hates it when people call her an interior designer. "I am a *whole environment designer*," she says. Whole environment design is when you take a perfectly ordinary person with ordinary-to-tacky taste and turn him into a "total design statement."

It works this way. Say you're a young executive moving into a new job, new town. You want to make a good impression. Mollie will help you find the right house. She'll decorate it for you. She'll help you choose the right car. She'll do your office. And then she'll do *you*. She'll arrange a new hairstyle, wardrobe, manicure. If you're overweight, she'll get you into an exercise program.

If you're married, she'll do your spouse, too. In fact, she'll tell you this is pretty much a necessity. If you're after a new look, you can't go around with the same old husband or wife.

Mollie hasn't "done" any children yet, but she will

help you choose the right pediatrician. Choosing the wrong pediatrician, she says, can send all sorts of bad messages about who you really *are*.

Mollie calls herself "M. Whitford Designs." It took a little while for the whole environment design idea to catch on, but once it did, she had to turn business away. She gets lots of calls from people about to move to Texas and California. Companies hire her to "do" all their new executives.

Back to Hal. Hal finished law school and almost went to work in a legal aid office representing poor people. Before his decent instincts could take over, Mollie stepped in and said, "No deal." I was only two when they had that fight, so I couldn't possibly remember it, but I've heard them rehash it so many times, I think I remember it.

Hal said, "It's my life." And Mollie said, "No, it's not just *your* life anymore. We have a child now. We have responsibilities. We can't just live on your dreams."

"Don't worry," Hal said. "You taught me to quit dreaming a long time ago."

They never *yelled* a lot. They just said terrible things to each other in very low voices.

They thought I wasn't listening. I was *always* listening. I could tell when things weren't right. Hal would smoke his pipe a lot in short irritated puffs and Mollie would wipe the kitchen counters over and over. That's when I would listen.

And all this time, they still loved each other. Every now and then, they would say so, and the bedroom door would close in the middle of a Saturday afternoon. Later, they would come out wearing their bathrobes, their cheeks all pink and their eyes bright and watery.

They *still* love each other, and that is the problem. All this commotion is coming about because they still love each other.

At least that's what Harvey says. She says most people who get divorced still love each other even if they don't even realize it. This creates a lot of confusion for everybody. Especially for the children.

Me, I don't understand why you leave someone you love. Maybe I'm stupid or something. But it seems to me love is hard enough to come by without just throwing it away when it starts to get a little inconvenient. So, I will never forgive Hal for leaving home, even though Mollie told him to.

That same day that Mollie announced she had to have her own life, and Hal made the crack about her not being satisfied with a whole damn planet, Mollie packed all his clothes and put them in the downstairs hall. She must have used every suitcase in the house, and while she packed she swore every swear word in the universe. She packed all his clothes except a few of his favorite funky old sweaters, which she pitched. I took them out of the trash when she wasn't looking and saved them for him.

When Hal got home that night, Mollie told him he was moving out. "Don't make a scene," she said.

And of course he didn't. He put the suitcases in the trunk of his car and drove off.

Just like that.

I watched his car all the way up Ashley Avenue until it turned onto Calhoun and disappeared.

Harvey wants to know how it felt.

It felt like the time I hit a home run and slammed head first into the tree that was home base. The air dissolved into little pieces until it was all black and I went falling down and down into the blackness, feeling like I was going to throw up, until everything was still.

I will never forgive Hal for leaving, and I will never forgive Mollie for telling him to.

FIVE

It is nothing out of the ordinary for my life to be tilted slightly sideways. I am not a straight-up-and-down, perpendicular kind of person.

It is natural, living here, to be slightly off-center. Almost all the old houses lean — some a little, others so much you wonder how anybody can live in them without getting dizzy. In my own house there is one bedroom you have to be careful in, the floor drops so, and when I was little, we used to roll marbles from one corner to the other to watch how fast they'd go. It's dangerous to sleep in there unless the bed is oriented exactly right. You can lose circulation in whichever part of your body is left hanging at the lower end.

My own bedroom is pretty straight, but even there

the walls wobble a little. And the view from my window is full of roofs that sag, columns that prop up porches about to fall into the street, and an old brick wall that leans dangerously toward the birdbath, which itself is not perpendicular to anything except maybe the crooked wisteria behind it.

It's part of the charm of the place that nothing is quite square. That's what Hal says.

Mollie is always trying to prop things up and get them straight.

There is something else about my town that makes for unsure footing, keeps us feeling on the edge as if we are about to fall off. We *are* right on the edge. The water surrounds us on three sides, the two rivers and the harbor that leads out to the ocean. And we are floating, barely, on the water underneath us. When it rains hard the streets are rivers, my backyard is a swamp. High tide eats the beaches and brings marsh mud onto Lockwood Boulevard, a street that was built on fill land. Underneath and out of sight are old cars, piles of tires, ancient refrigerators. An archaeologist's dream.

My house used to look out over the river, the last house on the tip of a little peninsula in what used to be a suburb. Once there was nothing across the street but marsh and long docks reaching out to the deeper water. I like to imagine what it must have been like to watch the sunset from our side porch, nothing out there but water and boats. No cars, no squat brick houses built in the nineteen-forties on land stolen from the river.

But even with the houses across the street, we are still on the edge. Water is everywhere, and always trying to get in. In the summertime everything is wet even when it doesn't rain. Our shoes get moldy in the closets.

If you see our town from above, from an airplane, it seems incredibly skinny and brave, surrounded by the sea. Water is everywhere, shining and silvery. Water is what will stay. It's as if the people who live here have just set up a campsite, with its sagging tents, along the rivers. It's only temporary.

So I am used to feeling a little disoriented and vulnerable. It's my natural state.

But lately, since Hal left, I've been dizzier than usual. It's been weeks now, and I still feel like I need to throw up.

Harvey asks me if I've talked to my friends about these feelings. I tell her I don't really have any friends anymore. Sure, I go to parties and talk on the telephone, but I don't tell anybody what's going on in my life. I'm afraid to talk to Evelyn. She'd tell me to snap out of it, to take charge and think positively. And I don't dare mention my problems to

Edward — he'd seize on this as an opportunity to get poetic and mushy. I almost wrote a letter to Tim. He wouldn't lecture me, or try to motivate me, and he definitely wouldn't get mushy. But he's got new friends now and a new life in Chicago. Why would he want to get a whiny letter from me?

I feel like I'm barely hanging on, and if I start to cry I'll lose my footing, slip off into the streets that are filling up with water, and go under for good.

Six

It was after two rainy weeks in July that the Blue Hydrangea Society decided to let boys in. Evelyn and I were getting on each other's nerves. Our mothers had quit playing tennis together, and the sleepy babysitter had finally stayed awake long enough to graduate from college, so we had no reason to stay together except the Blue Hydrangea. But we wondered if it wasn't beneath us — we were sixth graders then and in middle school — to be sneaking around the neighborhood after our parents had gone to bed, just to pick flowers and leave strange messages on people's front porches.

"It's just not cool anymore," Evelyn said, as if it had *ever* been cool. Everything Evelyn said was always so definite and dramatic, it was hard to disagree with her.

Sometimes I really hated Evelyn.

Evelyn had always been pretty, but by then, even though she was just barely eleven, she was positively gorgeous, like a tropical flower blossoming. And meanwhile I was trapped like a larva in my cocoon.

I remember coming home from school one day, after Evelyn had won the lead part in the spring play, and seeing myself sideways in the tall living room mirror. I could never bring myself to look straight on anymore — it was too awful, my whole self just *there* — but now even a side glance was horrifying. I burst into tears and ran upstairs to my room, throwing my book bag down with a thump. When Mollie came to see what was the matter, I couldn't help it, I just blurted out, "I *hate* Evelyn." Saying it made me cry even more, but it was true.

Mollie brought me a cool washcloth and a cup of mint tea. She sat at the foot of the bed and told me that girls who mature too early fade quicker. "By the time Evelyn is sixteen," she said, "she will be past her prime."

She kissed me on the cheek. "You, on the other hand, probably won't look your best until you're thirty." I did some quick subtraction in my head: nineteen more years to go. Not much of a comfort.

Anyway, if Evelyn hadn't come up with the idea of boys, the Blue Hydrangea would probably have died sooner. "We need some new blood," she said, "some inspiration. I think we need boys."

It occurred to me that maybe the need for boys was more Evelyn's than the Blue Hydrangea's. Evelyn is a person with powerful urges. But it was true that we were getting bored with each other and the Blue Hydrangea was suffering.

We chose Edward first. He was sort of nerdy and he was a poet. He lived around the corner with his father in a huge house that needed painting. His yard was overgrown, full of flowers that would be a good source for the Blue Hydrangea.

Evelyn decided I should be the one to send Edward a note at third period, because she said she thought he liked me a lot. This was typical Evelyn: if Edward laughed at us and our invitation to join a silly secret club, she could blame it all on me. After I sent the note, I realized how stupid it might sound, even to someone as unusual as Edward. *The Blue Hydrangea Society?* Leaving flowers and messages on people's front porches? I could almost hear him saying "Give me a break" under his breath.

But Edward didn't turn us down. He said he

thought it sounded "sensational." "Sensational" was one of those words Edward had a hard time saying without spitting, but he said it anyway, and I admired him for that. I also like the way he knotted his eyebrows when he read poetry, how serious and intense he was, as if every word he said made a difference to the future of the world.

After Edward came Tim Dawson. Tim lived in the projects, just a couple of blocks from my house. It might as well have been the other side of the universe. He went to our school, but he ate lunch with the other black kids, and after school he just disappeared back into the projects. It was like a line had been drawn around him which people like us couldn't cross.

Except for Edward. Edward and Tim had worked on a science project together and Edward thought Tim was going to be president someday, or if that didn't work out, at least a great actor. Tim had brains and good looks and could give oral book reports without shaking or stammering, with this deep voice that sounded older than he was. So Edward recruited Tim for the Blue Hydrangea.

The Blue Hydrangea was such a fragile thing, just an idea that if you thought about it too long seemed really stupid and silly, and I worried that boys might ruin it. Boys are not as complicated as girls, not as good at being subtle. If they don't like something, they just say so, and there is no way around it. But it turned out that after we admitted Edward and Tim, the Blue Hydrangea went on to do its greatest thing.

SEVEN

"We're working with our lawyers to come up with a plan for where you'll be living." That's what Mollie said.

She forgets I'm good at translating from I Don't Really Want to Talk About It, a language spoken almost exclusively by adults, into Get Real. And what Mollie said translates into "We're fighting over custody."

When I asked her point-blank if she and Hal were fighting over me, she said, "Not really. I think it's his way of showing his anger."

This was Mollie's way of not dealing with the fact that Hal, for the first time anybody could remember, wasn't doing exactly what Mollie wanted him to.

Could it be that Hal, who'd walked out the door

with the suitcases she'd packed for him, wouldn't just rent an apartment, pay some child support, and see me every other weekend? Of course not, she thought. Hal would never say "No." That's what Mollie thought.

So it wasn't until Hal hired Walter Martin that it occurred to her he might be bucking her plan. I had heard Hal talk about Martin. "One mean sonofabitch," he said. "He'll stop at nothing." Hal would pay him two hundred dollars an hour, and Martin would work round the clock to make Mollie miserable.

After Hal hired Martin, Mollie decided she needed someone more threatening than the fellow who handled her business stuff. So, she got Sonia Leonard. Mollie remembered how Hal had once called Sonia "a real ballbreaker." Just to get in to *see* Sonia, you had to pay a five-hundred-dollar consultation fee. Once you hired her, Sonia would unleash her whole staff on your spouse like a pack of hungry dogs, hounding him until they'd uncovered every embarrassing fact of his life, going back to infancy, and every note, letter, check, or other scrap of information he ever wrote. "Litigation by exhaustion," Hal had said. And Mollie remembered.

So now we have Martin *versus* Leonard, and it's going to be quite a battle.

The first round will be next Monday. They're going to have some kind of court thing to let the judge figure out where I should live until the case is over, which at this rate could be a long time.

Mollie assumes I want to keep living with her. She hasn't even bothered to ask. Hal just says, over and over, "This isn't your fault, honey. The grown-ups will just have to figure it out." He hasn't asked me what I want, either. And maybe that's a good thing, because I'm not so sure.

All I know is, I want things to be the way they were, even though they weren't always so great.

I want someone to fix my family.

EIGHT

Harvey says be honest. Don't hold back.

So, I will tell you how awful court was. This story is definitely rated R, for repulsive, rotten, and Rat. It's not for the squeamish.

First of all, nobody bothered to tell me I would have to be there. All of a sudden I wasn't going to school on Monday; I was going to court. Seems Walter Martin sent some kind of papers to Mollie commanding her to bring me. She showed it to me. I was "the minor child."

"You are hereby ordered to appear at the place and time below and bring with you the minor child."

So, there I was, sitting in this awful waiting room while I was supposed to be taking a math test. I definitely would have preferred the math test. You wouldn't *believe* the place. It wasn't the big fancy courthouse downtown, but a broken-down building a couple of blocks away. As Mollie would say, it looked like a business about to declare bankruptcy.

I think they made the waiting room really the pits to prepare you for what was coming next, which was even worse. I sat there between Mollie and another woman who was holding on to a runny-nosed baby. I slumped down in the beat-up plastic chair, trying to disappear. I closed my eyes and imagined Evelyn finding me here. She would act upbeat and friendly, as if nothing was wrong, but there would be that *edge* to her voice as she said, "*Hi*, Mac. Everything going okay?"

And Edward? What would Edward say? Probably something philosophical. Something maddening about how the human soul grows stronger in times of trouble.

But of course Evelyn and Edward didn't come to the Family Court. They were in math class, scribbling formulas — Evelyn probably on her way to an A-plus.

The woman and her runny-nosed baby were both crying by now. My own mother was dabbing at her eyes with a tissue but I could tell she wasn't really crying because her mascara wasn't running. Hal was huddled in a corner with Walter

Martin, going over some papers and looking very nervous.

A lot of other people were in there, too, all of them looking miserable in various ways, most of them looking poor. The walls were covered with old signs saying NO SMOKING, QUIET PLEASE, and IN CASE OF FIRE, USE STAIRS. This was interesting, because some people were smoking like crazy and grinding the butts into the dirty green-and-white tile floor, and the door to the stairway was chained shut.

Family Court is definitely a place full of contradictions. For example, you only come here when your family is falling apart.

Sonia Leonard came swooping in followed by a couple of young guys, one of whom was pushing a luggage cart filled with files. She went up to Walter Martin and slapped him on the back hard enough to knock him over. I guess this was supposed to be a friendly gesture, because Martin grinned a fake kind of grin and he didn't punch her out.

Sonia and Walter disappeared into the courtroom with Mollie and Hal and Sonia's two flunkies and the file cart. I wondered if all that paper was about my family, or if Sonia had a hundred other cases in court today.

I sat in the waiting room for what must have been

close to an hour, trying to mind my own business, but I couldn't help overhearing little snippets of other people's misery: "She done took the microwave *and* the washing machine."

"Least you don't have no kids. Mine got took over the weekend. Leftum by themselves for jus' a minute while we went to the store. Won't be long till they want to givum back. Least you don't have no kids."

Every so often a sheriff's deputy with a red face and a potbelly would come out and shout, "Quiet now, court's in session," but nobody paid any attention. And the women who worked behind the glass cage answering the phone and typing didn't pay any attention to the sideshow in front of them. Occasionally, someone would poke his head through the little hole they'd cut out to let the public speak to them, but whatever question was asked, the answer was never clear, and the clerks would point down the hall, sending the confused person to another court or another office, or just away.

I was beginning to think it didn't matter at all whether I would live with Mollie or with Hal as long as I could just get out of this place and never come back, when the potbellied deputy tapped me on the shoulder and said, now with a soft, kind voice that surprised me, "Miss, the Judge is ready for you now."

Nobody had said anything about me talking to the Judge. I didn't *want* to talk to the Judge. I wanted to go home, wherever home was going to be, and never set foot inside this place again.

NINE

I was taken down a long dark hall, past lots of little rooms jammed with clerks and computers and stacks of files, to the Judge's office. *JUDGE JUDGE'S CHAMBERS* the sign said. I found out later that before the Judge was a judge, he was Henry M. Judge, Lawyer. Rather than sound stupid saying "Judge Judge" over and over again, most of the lawyer's just called him "Your Honor."

The minute I walked into his office I could tell he was nuts. Not *bad* crazy, though. His craziness was kind of sweet. He was bald except for three strands of hair he had tried to comb over the bald spot, and he had big ears with droopy earlobes. His robe was sort of thrown over his regular clothes, not zipped up, and I could see what looked like a Grateful Dead T-shirt underneath.

"Sit down." He was chewing on something and pointing to a chair in front of his desk. It was one of those clunky old wooden office chairs with a curved back. It made me feel small.

His tongue moved whatever he was chewing over to one side of his mouth, which made his whole face look lopsided. "Before we begin, Margaret — it's Margaret, right?"

"They call me Mac."

"How old are you, Mac?"

"Thirteen."

"Eighth grade?"

"Yes, sir."

"Okay. How much do you know about what is going on here?"

"Not a whole lot, really. Nobody told me I had to say anything."

"That's not what I mean." He put his feet up on the desk and leaned back in his chair so far I thought he might fall over. "I mean, what's going on between your parents." The wad of whatever it was moved to the other side of his mouth.

"Oh, that." I decided to trust the guy. "I know a lot."

"Well, then, why don't you tell me what the deal is." He folded his arms and leaned back even farther, his chair bobbing back and forth.

"How long have we got?"

He threw his left arm up in the air to clear his watch from the sleeve of his robe and then brought it down very close to his face.

"Ten minutes. You'll have to get right to the heart of it. Pretend you're *not* a lawyer. Those fellows want to tell me about every hangnail their clients ever had. Proceed." He closed his eyes.

So I told him the story. The breakfast-table confrontation. Mollie packing the suitcases. Hal driving off. The snake hunt and the slippers. I had to leave out a lot of the background stuff, but he seemed to get the picture pretty fast. It occurred to me maybe he'd heard stories like this before.

"You know the guy?" His eyes were still closed.

"What guy?"

"The guy who owns the slippers."

"Oh, sure. That's Michael."

"Who's Michael?"

"Michael used to be one of Mollie's clients. She did him over."

He sat up now, looking interested. "So is there more than one? I mean, is your mother . . ."

"No. Look, it's more complicated than you think."
I felt sorry for Judge Judge. Hearing this sort of stuff
all day must be really depressing.

"Who takes care of you?" He was scribbling on a
pad now.

"What do you mean?"

He seemed impatient: "You know, who takes you
to the doctor, sits up with you when you're sick,
tucks you in at night, helps you with your homework,
runs out for poster paper in the middle of the night
when you remember you've got a science project
due tomorrow, et cetera, et cetera, et cetera." He
smacked the wad of whatever with each et cetera.

"They both do." I could see I wasn't helping him
out any.

"Well, would you feel better living with your mom
or your dad? I mean just temporarily, until this
whole mess is straightened out?"

"Maybe I don't want to live with either one of
them until they can start behaving themselves."

His enormous Adam's apple moved under his
throat like a rock, and I thought he might swallow
the wad.

"I understand you're seeing a therapist. Is she
okay?"

"Harvey? She's okay. She does pretty well for
somebody who doesn't know much about kids."

"This Michael guy, does he stay over?" He was looking at a piece of paper, trying to act like he wasn't reading it while he was talking to me.

"I don't think so. I go to bed at ten, but I don't think so." I was mad at Mollie, but not mad enough to sink her ship with one torpedo. I was hoping Judge Judge would forget about the slippers.

He stood up and looked at his watch. Our ten minutes were up. He turned to the window, and burped. While his back was turned I got a peek at the paper. It was legal-looking and signed by Mary Rattick, hereinafter The Rat. Mary Rattick is, or was, Mollie's best friend. I had to read fast, so I missed a lot, but according to Mary Rattick, one Michael McMenamin was cohabiting with my mother.

Judge Judge turned around. "I'm going to appoint a Guardian for you. You'll like her. We call her a guardian *ad litem*, fancy Latin lawyer-talk, but it means she'll be your protector in this custody case. She'll look out for you, help me figure out what's best for you."

He stood up. I stood up. "Her name is Henrietta Porter LePage Middleton. Don't let it throw you. She's not at all like she sounds." He came around the desk and put his hand on my shoulder. "Take care, kid. Call me if you need me. You'll make it through this okay. You've got your head screwed on tight."

The two armies were camped outside the Judge's chambers, waiting for me to come out. Mollie and Sonia Leonard and her flunkies, Hal and his lawyer, all trying to read my face. There was only one thing I had to say:

"Mary Rattick is a Rat."

TEN

Harvey says I need to let my anger out. I don't need to worry about hurting people's feelings. I can say whatever I want to.

Maybe she thinks I am inhibited or something. She's wrong about that. I say pretty much what I want to anyway, therapist or no therapist. But she's right about my not wanting to hurt Hal and Mollie's feelings. They're acting really nuts right now. They bum me out about every fifteen seconds, but I can't bring myself to say it to their faces. I honestly think it would drive them over the edge.

I would like to tell Hal how much I wish he would stop trying to look pitiful. When we all lived together we had a rule: "No moping." You could cry, yell, kick things, or whatever, but you couldn't just sit around

43

and mope. Mollie used to say, "Moping is not productive." It was one of the few things she and Hal agreed on.

So I would like to tell Hal to quit moping. I wish he would tell jokes the way he used to, even though most of them were stupid. I wish he would laugh out loud like he used to, even though it's embarrassing when he makes so much noise in the movie theater. I wish he would dance around the kitchen with me, to old-timey music. Now he seems so serious and he is always bringing work home, talking about how money is tight, or poring over the piles of legal papers Walter Martin faxes to him every day. He seems so sad and so old I feel I am visiting somebody with a terminal disease.

And I would like to talk to Mollie about the Perfect Mother problem. Lately she's spending an awful lot of time with me. I mean compared to when we all lived together. She does a lot of cooking, very balanced meals with green vegetables. She wakes me up on Saturday morning to do things like go to the art museum. God, it's terrible.

I also wish she would quit trying to hide the Michael thing from me and just deal with it. I don't have to be much of a detective to figure he's here a lot after I go to bed. I come down to the kitchen before Mollie's awake and find two wine glasses on the counter. Once, a couple of days ago, there was a strange toothbrush on the bathroom sink. And the pillowcase on Mollie's bed smells like men's cologne. It's really a pain the way we both have to pretend Michael doesn't exist.

I would like to yell at *both* of my parents for making me give up Bal, the boa constrictor. He was too big, they said, to haul back and forth, and he would get lonely without me if he stayed put. So I had to give him to the biology professor who lives down the street, and I only have visitation rights.

Most of all I would like to talk to them about bugging me for information. They're both pretty sneaky about it. For instance, Hal will say, "How's your mom doing? I hope she isn't too lonely when you're over here with me." This of course is supposed to make me think he really cares about how she's doing, but what he really wants is for me to tell him about The Other Man.

Or Mollie will ask me about Hal's apartment. She does this as if she's just the designer interested in his décor. What she really wants to know is whether he's setting up a separate life on a permanent basis, with nice furniture and all, or whether it looks like something temporary.

Harvey says this is all normal. It will get better. But in the meantime, she says, I have a right to be angry and she will help me deal with it. She says my parents are so busy dealing with themselves at this point they aren't capable of dealing with me.

I am trying to remember a time when they *were* capable of dealing with me.

ELEVEN

Harvey reminds me that other people's families aren't so perfect either. This is sometimes hard to remember, because the place I live in is so beautiful you can't imagine anything too awful happening in it. Walk down King Street toward the harbor, and you'll see what I mean. The homes look like dollhouses, each one painted a different pastel color, the brick ones neatly decorated with pastel shutters. The yards are neat and green and the windowboxes are miniature gardens spilling over with carefully chosen colors.

For example, about a block away from the harbor there is a pink house with gray-green shutters. If you stand at the iron gate on the street and look through to the backyard, you can see a water fountain surrounded by reclining angels, sweet little children minding their own business. It's enough to make you think this is a perfect world, this house and this yard, and nothing bad ever happens in it.

Harvey tells me to think about the real people who live there. She's right. Helen Smith and her four sisters are certainly not angelic. Helen got kicked out of school for mouthing off to the principal — after several warnings — and her sisters have followed along in her tradition of trouble, each one doing worse things than the one before her. Now some prep school up north is making a fortune off the Smith family.

And what about the members of the Blue Hydrangea? asks Harvey. The Blue Hydrangea is defunct, I say. Tell me anyway, she insists. So I start with Evelyn.

She lives right around the corner, and you can get into her backyard by crawling through the hole in the fence from my backyard. Her mother is a fanatic about roses and her whole yard is one swirling maze of rosebushes, all different colors. Evelyn's mother has definitely missed her calling. She should have run a garden store or been a farmer. Instead she sells office furniture.

Maybe that's why she takes so many nerve pills, because it's so awful leaving her beautiful rose garden and going out to sell office furniture. She lives in two worlds. I've seen her popping pills at eight in the morning when she's driving carpool. But more likely Evelyn's mother takes pills because Evelyn's father is such a mess. He stays home now because his business went bankrupt, and I've heard Mollie and Hal whispering about how he might go to jail for doing things too complicated for me to understand.

Evelyn's parents are running out of money, but they keep pretending they are doing fine, and so does Evelyn. She is always smiling, and even though I sometimes hate her I have to admire her acting skills. One day she will win an Academy Award.

And Edward. Edward and his family were always just barely hanging together anyway, but then his mother had her accident. She wrote fantasy books for grownups, weird stories about microscopic people who live in a microscopic society just under the earth's crust and communicate in music instead of language. She wrote in the attic with an old record player playing Bach tunes over and over, and as the years went by she just got further and further away from reality until, as Edward says, she just couldn't bear to live anymore, and stepped out in front of a fast-moving car on the Cooper River Bridge. She's been in a nursing home now for three years.

Edward is creative like his mother, but I worry that he will get *too* creative, if you know what I mean. There is a thin line between being creative and being crazy.

Tim lives in Chicago now. But back in the days of the Blue Hydrangea, his family was probably the most normal, even though they live in the projects and you would think from reading the papers that nothing normal ever happens there. Before Tim left for Chicago, he shared a second floor apartment with his grandmother, his mother, and his little brother.

Tim's grandmother ruled the household. She was tough, but friendly, and when she hugged you, you felt really hugged. She never said things she didn't mean, so when she gave you a compliment you knew you deserved it. She made great biscuits and the minute you opened the door to the stairwell you could smell something good cooking. She said she never stopped cooking because with Tim growing so much he was always wanting something to eat.

Tim's grandmother took care of his little brother while his mother went off to work. When Tim's mother left for her job at the hospital in the early morning, she looked good in her starched white uniform, but by the time she came home in the afternoon she looked tired and defeated.

The missing piece of Tim's family was his father, who lived in Chicago and only came home three or four times a year. Tim didn't seem to think there was anything abnormal about this. He adored his father and when they got together, they talked about what Tim was going to do when he grew up. Tim's father told him to stay in school, to go to college so he wouldn't end up driving a taxi.

Tim's father was tall and handsome and played saxophone in a jazz band when he wasn't driving his taxi. But Tim's grandmother wasn't charmed. "I say it like it is," she said to me, "That man got no more sense than a bug in June. He just lights here for a night or two, and then he flits off to wherever."

Now that I think about it, I wonder if *anybody* is really normal, and if there is even one family in this town that doesn't have some deep dark secret.

TWELVE

Let me tell you about Henrietta Porter LePage Middleton. Remember, she's the one Judge Judge said would look out for my best interests. Harvey, I *swear* I am telling the truth, because you are not going to believe this.

She came to pick me up on a bicycle. Not just a bicycle. A bicycle built for two. This seventy-something old woman with a funny hat and huge black shoes comes riding down Ashley Avenue, the wrong way, on a double bicycle. I was looking out of the crack between the living room shutters, waiting for her, so I saw the grand arrival. I could have died.

I consider myself an individualist, you know, and I don't really mind not being like everybody else, but I would never have imagined myself being picked up by this very unusual-looking old lady on a double bicycle.

Henrietta (we'll skip the other two names for now) Middleton wore a red beret, big black tie-up shoes, and a jacket that flew out behind her like a sail. But she introduced herself with fine Old Charleston manners and acted as if everything was just as normal as it could be. No apologies for the bicycle. In fact, I think she thought she was doing me a great honor.

"The late Dr. Middleton and I used to ride this all the time," she said, as if I knew who Dr. Middleton was. Maybe her husband. She seemed to presume I knew everything about her. This is a peculiar trait of Old Charlestonians. They always talk about people you never heard of as if they were your best friends. It's annoying, because you're too embarrassed to admit you have no idea what they're talking about, and you're left in the dark.

I could have made a scene, but I decided that if this old lady had enough nerve to ride this bicycle, so did I. So I got on behind her.

It may very well be that Judge Judge has appointed Henrietta Middleton to look out for my best interests, but if so, they are my spiritual best interests, because my bodily interests are definitely ignored. And if I ride with her many more times I won't have to worry about my body at all.

She doesn't seem to notice cars or stoplights. Buses don't impress her either. She just keeps moving. Fortunately she seems to have established some sort of reputation for reckless biking, because most people get out of her way pretty fast. We had only a few *real* close calls between Mollie's house and hers. Screeching brakes, lots of swearing, etc. She never noticed.

Henrietta's house is as strange as she is. But kind of neat. It's in what Mollie would call "a transitional neighborhood," meaning all the houses are old, some are falling down, and some have been fixed up by Yankees who move down here and think they're going to make a fortune in real estate. This mansion was built in 1840. It has never been renovated, or at least not in the last hundred years.

You open this huge iron gate, very fancy but rusty, and go into the yard. There are flowers everywhere, but in no particular order, nothing like the little beds in complicated designs we have in our backyard. There are two big oak trees, the kind you almost never see except in the country, with their long limbs dipping low to the ground.

You go up the steps to the porch, which is high off the ground and as wide as most houses. Inside the place is a sort of dignified catastrophe. Chunks of plaster have fallen from the ceiling, the wallpaper is ancient, and the floors haven't been refinished in decades, but despite all this the place looks important. The furniture is dark and big and old, the cloth satiny and still showing some of its original pattern. In the dining room there is an immense table and a matching sideboard loaded up with silver that's polished to the hilt. I am talking about big bowls and pitchers and things. A thief's dream, and the windows in this place don't even close all the way.

The best part is the kitchen. You go down from the dining room two or three steps onto a brick floor. Big bricks like you can't buy anymore. And a fireplace covering one whole wall. No dishwasher, no microwave, just the basics.

Mrs. Middleton asked me what I would like to drink. "I have juice," she said, "or milk." I asked her what she was going to have, and she said she thought she'd have a little sherry. I said I'd like some sherry, too.

She didn't skip a beat. She poured honey-colored liquid into two perfectly gorgeous crystal glasses and led me out to the porch. And there we sipped our sherry and talked about everything in the world.

We talked about art. She told me her favorite artist was some guy named Miró, and when I told her I didn't know much about Miró (true, because I didn't know a *thing* about Miró) she went into the house and brought out a fat art history book full of pictures. The ones by Miró looked like something you might find under a microscope, but they were pretty neat. She asked me who my favorite artist was. I told her Michelangelo. I like the hand of God reaching down to Adam in the Sistine Chapel. She agreed and said she had once really *seen* the Sistine Chapel.

We talked about books and music. Mrs. Middleton seems to know a lot about almost everything. She has met a lot of famous people. She told me how Ralph Waldo Emerson had once spent a night in her house. "Before I lived here, of course." *But not too long before,* I thought.

I didn't really like the sherry. It made me feel funny. It was too thick and sweet. But Mrs. Middleton seemed to like hers, and she had another glass before we left to go back to Mollie's house. I wondered if you could get picked up for drunk driving on a bicycle.

When she dropped me off she said, "We'll get together again." Only then did I realize she hadn't asked me about Mollie or Hal, the divorce, Judge Judge, or any of that stuff.

THIRTEEN

Judge Judge judged not. That's right, Harvey, he opted out. He split me right down the middle, gave half to Mollie and half to Hal. I spend one week with my mother, the next week with my father. So nobody won the first round, and nobody lost. We're *all* mad, even though it's only temporary.

Harvey, I figured he was trying to be King Solomon. You remember, the one who threatened to chop the baby in half with his sword, just to see which mother loved him enough to give him up, because that would be the real mother.

But it didn't work. I got cut in half.

At first, it was kind of exciting. I mean, I had my room at Mollie's house (when I call it Mollie's house, Hal clenches his teeth and his jaw twitches) and also a bedroom all my own at Hal's apartment. He let me furnish it with funky stuff from Polk's Flea Market — an old brass bed, a wicker chair, a chest of drawers with an ancient wavy mirror, and a Bohemian-looking rug with long white hair. All very impractical, the kind of stuff Mollie has apoplexy over. But I have a flair for pulling things together, maybe inherited from her, a talent for organizing the bizarre.

After the first couple of weeks the hassle started to get to me. I couldn't remember where I was supposed to *be*. I mean, don't you think it's natural for a person to have one room, one bed, one house? I forget now which house I'm supposed to go to after school. And if I leave my science book at Mollie's house, there is this enormous problem in the morning when Hal has to drive me over there to get it before school. I'm supposed to cut my ties with her when I'm with him.

It all looked so logical when they showed me the calendar. A week here, a week there, with some juggling around for holidays and birthdays.

But how do I explain to my friends that *this* week I'm with my mother, who goes ballistic if I get a phone call after nine P.M., but *next* week I'm with Hal, and it's okay to call as late as eleven? I *don't* explain. It's too complicated and embarrassing. Even if I told Evelyn and Edward, who know me better than anyone else, they wouldn't understand how a thirteen-year-old can get sent back and forth like a Ping-Pong ball, a week here and a week there.

I can't hide the fact that Mollie and Hal are separated — that's no big deal these days, anyway — but I try to pretend I have some control over my own whereabouts.

"Cool," says Evelyn, when I tell her I can come and go as I please.

"Yeah," says Edward, "Your parents must be really *mature*."

I think it's starting to drive Mollie and Hal crazy, too. When I'm with Mollie for "her" week, she feels as though she has to spend every waking minute with me. All this quality time is killing her. Poor Michael McMenamin must be desperate, a week on and a week off like that. It's exhausting for my mother, but she's trying her best to follow Sonia Leonard's instructions. And Hal is so miserable after his week without me that I feel guilty if I want to spend the night over with friends on one of "his" nights. It's bad for Mollie and Hal, but worse for me.

My digestive system is getting a total workout. On "Mollie's week," I am stuffed with green vegetables. I have plenty of fiber and breakfasts fit for a construction worker. Then I get to Hal's and make up for it with fast food galore — a French-fry fantasy — and for breakfast the kind of cereal I have always wanted: bright colors, a prize in every box, and sugar as the first ingredient.

So Judge Judge's compromise is making us all miserable, but Mollie and Hal won't admit it. They're even breathing a sigh of relief.

Half a kid isn't great, but it's better than none at all.

FOURTEEN

Harvey's assignment for the day: Describe your appearance to a total stranger. Also your parents. What do they look like?

I'll try to be objective.

Most people think Mollie is beautiful, but Mollie doesn't. She says her nose holds her back. She has no idea how discouraging it is for me to have my absolutely gorgeous mother going around complaining about her almost-perfect looks. Sometimes I think I will kill her if she whines one more time about her nose. Her nose is long and thin and just because it doesn't turn up a little at the end, she complains about it. I'm surprised she hasn't had it "done" already.

Mollie has *real* blond hair, great skin, and enormous brown eyes that are dazzlers. She is tall and skinny in a healthy sort of way.

Hal gets more handsome every year. At least *I* think so. He's got this very patrician profile, he's tall, and he stands up straight all the time. In old photographs he looks too severe, but now that he's put on a little weight, his face has filled out and he's friendlier looking. He has these great furry eyebrows and sad gray eyes. His hair is getting white around his ears and a little thin on top.

Given this divine genetic material, I don't know how I could have turned out to look, well, like *me*. I'm short for my age, and slightly overweight. Mollie keeps telling me my pudginess is just a stage, and I'll grow out of it. She's been saying this for as long as I can remember, and instead of growing out of it, I seem to be growing *into* it.

My hair has no redeeming qualities. It is dull brown and absolutely straight and shapeless, except in humid weather, when it develops this stubborn curl on the right side only, making me look off-balance. We have tried perming it, to give it some shape, but after eighty-five hours of being poisoned by a perm solution that must have come from a toxic waste dump, my hair was still determined to be straight. "She has impervious follicles," said the guy who was doing my hair.

I do have great eyes. They are large and almond-shaped and I might even say exotic, except it is hard to make the case that anything about such an ordinary-looking person could be exotic.

Since I was not born with much to work with, I have to be creative. I like hats: hats with big brims that droop down over my face and make my eyes look even more mysterious, berets in bright colors, and, for special occasions, antique old-lady hats with feathers and netting. Mollie says I overdo the hat thing. It embarrasses her that I call attention to myself. Only once, a couple of months ago, did she understand the usefulness of hats.

It was a bad *bad* hair day. Everywhere, there are good hair days and bad hair days. In Charleston, there are some bad *bad* hair days — wet and humid and hot. They give hair a bad attitude, and even the best hair will look wimpy or frizzy.

Anyway, it was a superbad hair day, and Mollie had an appointment with a new client. The more she brushed, the sadder her hair looked. She got positively frantic. Finally, I suggested a hat, and we found the perfect felt one, simple and sophis-ticated — I'd bought it at the second-hand store a couple of weeks before — into which she tucked all her bad hair. She looked terrific.

It is one of the very few times I could remember that Mollie ever listened to me.

FIFTEEN

Harvey asks me to tell her about the time, other than now, when I have been most afraid.

It was the time the Blue Hydrangea Society got arrested.

Mr. Murgrave, our sixth grade French teacher, had just gotten fired. One day we walked into class and instead of Mr. Murgrave there was this young woman substitute who spoke French with a Southern accent. All the syllables were drawn out so long it was like she couldn't bear to let them go. We all snickered and passed notes back and forth all that French period. We assumed Mr. Murgrave would be back the next day, that he had one of his colds again and was staying home in bed with a couple of boxes of Kleenex and a stack of papers to correct.

But later that day the rumors were flying. Mr. Murgrave would not be coming back. He was really sick this time, in intensive care at St. Luke's Hospital with the nuns looking after him and priests coming and going. He had written his last will and testament. Whatever was wrong with him was something none of the other teachers wanted to talk about, but it was going to kill him.

Mr. Murgrave was my favorite teacher. He was really strict and when you came into his class you knew you were going to be serious about French. He had lived in France for a year and he spoke with this wonderful accent that made me feel like I wanted to move to Paris. Once we crossed the threshold into his classroom, we couldn't use another word of English until we left forty-five minutes later.

Mr. Murgrave loved France, and everything French. He told us about Paris, the Côte d'Azur, Normandy, about Notre Dame and Chartres and the vineyards, about Monet's garden at Giverny. He told us how when he was a poor student he hitchhiked all over France living off wine, bread, and cheese. Lately he had been wearing a funny little black beret in class. It did a good job of hiding his bald head.

I went into the assistant principal's office at lunch time to find out the truth about Mr. Murgrave. "What's wrong with Mr. Murgrave?" I asked. The school secretary turned red and suggested I talk to the principal about it. So I did.

"It's not something we're free to discuss, Margaret. It's a very unfortunate situation, to say the least. But I'm sure Miss Apple will do a wonderful job taking over for Mr. Murgrave. She has her master's, and she's very enthusiastic."

"But she can't speak French," I said before I even thought about it. What I really meant was, "Nobody could ever take Mr. Murgrave's place."

That night we convened an emergency meeting of the Blue Hydrangea. It was January, and too cold for outdoor meetings, but we didn't have any choice because none of our parents would let us meet on a school night. We waited until midnight, when all our households were sleeping soundly, to sneak out. We met in the dark next to the remains of the old museum, where the four columns and the steps that used to lead up into the building are still standing.

We were only a block away from the hospital.

"I can't believe they fired him just because he's sick," I said.

"You guys want to know what *really* happened?" said Evelyn, and we all leaned forward, shivering. I had thrown my coat on over my pajamas but forgotten my gloves.

"Shoot," said Tim.

"Mr. Murgrave has AIDS. Remember those purple splotches he got all over his face?"

We all nodded. I was beginning to feel sick.

Evelyn continued, "When he kept being absent so much, they asked for a copy of his medical records and he kept putting them off. He told them he was getting better, and it would only be a couple of weeks before he was his old self again. They fired him because he wouldn't turn over the records."

I was breathing harder now and my breath danced in the glow from the streetlight. I rubbed my hands together and blew on them.

"We need to make a visit," Tim said.

It was going to be tough finding flowers at this time of year. There had been a hard freeze a couple of days before, and almost everything was shriveled and brown by now.

We shouldn't have done what we did next, but this was an emergency. We walked half a block and lifted four pots of poinsettias from the window boxes outside the old people's home on Calhoun Street. They were probably left over from Christmas, we said, and anyway, they'd been burned by the freeze and were beginning to look a little ragged. Maybe, Evelyn said, we were even helping out the maintenance man by getting rid of them.

Edward called the hospital information desk from

a pay phone on the corner. We all got in the phone booth with him to keep from freezing to death. He made his voice sound especially adult, and he put on a French accent. "So sorry to disturb you this late at night," he said, doing a really good job of it, "but I am Monsieur Murgrave's cousin calling from Paris. Would you give me his room number, *s'il vous plait*? He mouthed "Four-O-One" to us.

By now the phone booth was beginning to feel really crowded. I burst out laughing because it was so ridiculous, the four of us and the pots of poinsettias in our ready-made steamy greenhouse on the corner of Rutledge and Calhoun in the middle of the night.

"I don't know what you think is so funny," Evelyn said, in that way she has of sounding superior.

"Sorry," I said, before I could think about it, though I really wasn't.

But I'm getting too long-winded. Harvey wants to know what happened next.

The Blue Hydrangea got arrested on the fourth floor of St. Luke's Hospital. We had sneaked past the nurses' desk and down the hall to Room 401, opened the door that said ABSOLUTELY NO VISITORS, and gone inside, where Mr. Murgrave lay on the bed hooked up to a million tubes and machines with blinking lights. He was definitely not in good shape, but his eyes were open, and I caught what I thought was a wink.

We put the pots of poinsettias on the bedside table. Edward had just finished writing "Nous t'aimons" (with Evelyn's mother's lipstick) on the mirror opposite Mr. Murgrave's bed, when two guards came in with guns drawn. It was a little bit of an overreaction, if you ask me, but I guess those guys didn't have much excitement around the hospital, and when anything like a break-in presented itself, they went into high gear, even if it was only four kids in their pajamas leaving flower-messages.

The hospital guards called the police, and we were hauled home one by one.

I don't even need to tell you what it was like to stand there on my own front doorstep with a cop, like some common criminal, waiting for my parents to answer the doorbell.

But more about that later.

SIXTEEN

I had my second meeting with my Guardian today, at the new Charleston Museum. That's where Henrietta Middleton works, back in a dark little cubicle behind the mummies.

She is too old to be working, she says, but too young to quit. She would be restless at home and would get into more trouble. If she retired, there would be more time to write letters to the editor and organize demonstrations.

She writes lots of letters to the editor. When Dr. Middleton was alive, she says, he used to edit them and throw the really obnoxious ones away; but now that he is gone, there is no one to keep her under control, and she writes exactly what she thinks — which is not exactly what everybody else thinks.

She especially likes criminals. She is always pushing for some fellow with a long record to get out on parole because he's learned to read and she's found him a job. She's goes absolutely *nuts* whenever they're about to execute somebody up at the state penitentiary, and she rides the bus up there to demonstrate against the death penalty.

She is not afraid of *anything*, she says, except ignorance. She likes to teach people how to read. She says she wishes all the people who already know how to read would learn how to *think*.

Henrietta Middleton is often the subject of gossip. Once, she said, the neighbors started a story that she had a murderer living in her attic bedroom. This was absolutely untrue because the fellow wasn't a murderer at all, but a common housebreaker who had never laid a hand on anybody and needed a place to stay, just temporarily, when he got out of prison. He was quite pleasant and never bothered anybody, and he'd helped her with the gardening.

Mollie says Mrs. Middleton use to be a pinko. I had to ask Hal what this meant. He was furious. "Of course she isn't a communist," he said. "She's just outspoken. And besides which," he said, "your mother shouldn't try to undermine your Guardian."

What Hal doesn't realize is that it would take more than Mollie to undermine Henrietta Porter LePage Middleton.

Back to the museum. Apparently they have tried to retire Mrs. Middleton, but she is just not retirable. So they have given her the little back room and made her promise to stay in there doing her cataloging and writing thank-you notes.

The thank-you notes are to all the well-meaning people who donate their antiques, great-grandmother's dolls and great-great-uncle Harry's uniform from the War Between the States. The museum never turns down anything. They just put most of it in storage and have Mrs. Middleton write one of her thank-you notes. She showed me one:

"Dear Mr. and Mrs. Jones, The Museum of the City of Charleston wishes to thank you for your very generous donation of pottery which you found while digging in your garden. It was wonderful of you to part with these historic pieces, and you can be sure they will be treasured by the museum." Sure, the blue-and-white pieces, all yellowed and broken, were old. But they were dime store variety dinnerware.

After she has written the thank-you note, Mrs.

Middleton puts the china pieces in a little plastic bag, tags it with a date and number, and makes a corresponding card for her card box.

The museum does have some neat stuff. When you walk in the door, you look up and there is a gigantic whale skeleton hanging from the ceiling. You can imagine how Jonah must have felt. And there are some great old dresses, very fancy and lacy, on short mannequins with waists so tiny you wonder whether the original owners had room for digestive systems.

But the best thing is the mummies. Of course, mummies have nothing to do with Charleston, except that some adventurous Charlestonian must have robbed a Pharaoh's tomb when you could still get away with that kind of thing.

What I like about the mummies is that they are so *dead* but still so dignified. They lie there in a sort of trance, their hands folded over their chests as if they're waiting for a curtain to open. I like to imagine how they would look standing upright, still and serious, like in the beginning of some modern dance.

So in my second visit with my Guardian I spent an hour learning how to write thank-you notes. I also complained a lot. But she asked for it.

"*Well?*" she said, as if I knew what she was after, which of course I did.

"Not good," I answered. She knew I was talking about the schedule.

"I don't know whether there is anything we can do about it, but tell me what's bothering you, and perhaps I'll think of something." This is what I like about Henrietta Middleton, that she makes no promises, and she never tries to make a bad situation sound good.

I told her about the week with Mollie and the week with Hal. I think she knew already, because she didn't seem at all surprised.

I told her I felt this whole mess wasn't my fault, but I was the one who was getting really screwed. The minute I said "screwed" I knew I shouldn't have, because even though Henrietta Middleton is an outspoken person, she is outspoken in a genteel way, and *screwed* is not part of her vocabulary. She patted my hand and said, "I know, it must be *very* disorienting."

"Yes," I said. I made her promise she wouldn't send a letter to the editor, or a telegram to the governor. She laughed.

But I could tell she had a plan.

SEVENTEEN

One of the worst things about all this mess with Mollie and Hal and me is that it's messing up springtime.

I exaggerate a lot, but I do truly believe that Charleston in the springtime is the finest place on earth.

Somewhere around mid-March we start sleeping with the windows open even though it's still chilly. Early in the morning the birds start singing in a new way, with a lot of energy, as if they're spreading the word that winter is over and everything is going to be absolutely *terrific* for the next couple of months.

The fig tree below my window puts out its first leaves, all curled up like green babies who aren't quite ready to wake up from a nap. Then about a week later they uncurl and stretch and become real fig leaves, bright green and fuzzy.

My fig tree is a survivor of The Hurricane. Around here you don't have to say *which* hurricane. They know. Most people have long since repaired their houses and gotten their yards cleaned up, but hardly a day goes by without some mention of The Hurricane. Even if you didn't speak English, you could tell they were talking about *It*. Their heads drop, they talk slower and in low voices, then they shake their heads back and forth understandingly. At the end of what I call a Hurricane Recollection Session, people stand quiet and still for a minute. It's as if somebody really important died, and they are all related to him.

Mollie is the only person I know who didn't seem fazed by The Hurricane. I mean, sure, when we came back to town the day after, she was as bummed out as anybody — we had marsh mud and dead shrimp and the remains of our vegetable garden in the living room, and the back half of the roof had been peeled off, leaving a sort of gigantic skylight, which was great until it started raining and didn't stop for three days.

But you have to remember that Mollie gets energized by renovation. Dealing with roofers, plumbers, painters, and so forth turns her on. She actually *likes* to pick out wallpaper, and so The Hurricane was the opportunity of a lifetime. People all over town were calling her, begging for help. Most normal Charlestonians were immobilized by the mess all around them. They just stood around shaking their heads and muttering over their Sterno cookers.

Anyway, my fig tree was ripped up by the roots, turned over sideways, and then given up for dead and sawed off into a stump by the guys Hal hired to clean up the backyard. It wasn't really their fault; I mean, the place was a jungle — trees down everywhere and mud up to your knees. They were just trying to clear a path to the garage.

If I hadn't pulled what remained of the fig tree upright and tucked its roots back under the mud, it would have been a goner. It's only been three years now, and already the tree is higher than the back door. Whenever I feel really lousy, I look out my window and commune with the fig tree. It got beheaded, and I only got chopped in half.

But back to springtime. In Charleston, it's almost too much to bear. Every hour in a classroom is torture. In the afternoon, when school lets out (and if you are lucky and there isn't too much homework), you can ride around on your bicycle all afternoon and pretend there is no tomorrow.

But if your parents are getting a divorce and fighting over you, you worry a lot about tomorrow.

Usually I don't think much about The Future. Evelyn and Edward worry a lot about what they're going to be when they grow up. Evelyn wants to be an actress, but thinks maybe she ought to have a fall-back plan. Edward is torn between being an astronaut and being a philosopher. Tim will end up being president, even if he *did* get arrested, but he'll probably have to get a regular job somewhere along the way.

I am the only one who doesn't have a plan. Usually it doesn't bother me. I especially do not worry about The Future during these first perfect spring days, because I am smart enough to realize that perfect days are few and far between, and The Future can wait.

But this April, when I ride my bike after school, I have a weird feeling that despite the sun on my back and the birds singing and the flowers everywhere, the whole world is *not* perfect, and I had better be careful, because something terrible could happen when I am not looking.

EIGHTEEN

Harvey wants me to go back to that time, two years ago, when the Blue Hydrangea got arrested.

It seems funny now, but it wasn't funny then. Hal came down in his pajamas, rubbing his eyes and turning on the porch light so the whole neighborhood could see me and the cop standing there, the cop clutching the collar of my jacket as if I were going to try to run away or something.

"You Mr. Whitford?" Hal nodded, so taken aback he forgot to ask us to step inside. "We picked this one up with a gang of juveniles. Breaking and entering St. Luke's Hospital."

"Gang of juveniles" had this very evil sound about it, not at all like the Blue Hydrangea Society. By this time Hal had invited Lieutenant Capers in for a cup of coffee, which the lieutenant declined. He had let go of my collar. We sat around the dining room table. I could hear Mollie thumping around upstairs, probably looking for her exercise outfit so she wouldn't have to come down in her bathrobe.

Lieutenant Capers tore off the top sheet of the little pad on which he'd scribbled the charges against me, and handed it to Hal. "I'm deviating from standard procedure here," said the lieutenant. "If I wrote her up for the maximum she'd have to spend the night at the detention center. That's no place for a girl like yours, from a nice family and all." I was beginning to feel a little better. At least I was out of the real criminal category.

"She'll have to attend counseling for the un-governable. Then the solicitor will probably drop the charges." Lieutenant Capers seemed to like all these official-sounding words. He stood up, looking very large and very official. "Tell you what, Mr. Whitford, if this was my girl I'd make sure she didn't hang around that kid from the projects anymore. That one is going nowhere but trouble."

Mollie came into the dining room just in time to hear about "that kid from the projects." Sure enough, she had on her best exercise outfit, the blue one with the tight stretchy pants and the match-ing T-shirt that covered her thighs. Mollie has a thing about her thighs. She's always talking about cellulite.

She introduced herself to Lieutenant Capers, and once she'd figured out what was going on she started to dab at her eyes with a table napkin. Thank goodness the lieutenant was already headed for the door. I didn't want him to go into any more detail about my criminal activity.

After the officer left, Hal made himself some coffee and sat in the living room staring at the wall. He sighed. "We'll discuss this in the morning, Mac," he said in a very pained way, so that I felt sorrier for him than I did for myself.

After I went to bed, I could hear them talking in low voices about how to deal with me.

Mollie cried. "I don't see how you can possibly be so calm about this," she said. "She's our *daughter*."

And Hal said, "Let's not overreact. I had a few close calls with the law when I was about her age. If my parents had known what I was up to . . ."

"I can't *believe* you're acting this way," Mollie said, her voice loud enough now for me to hear her clearly. "It's almost as if you're *proud* she got picked up by the police. And I suppose it doesn't bother you at all that she's hanging out with kids from the projects?"

"I just don't think we should jump to conclusions,

Mollie. She's always been such a good kid. We'll give her a serious talking-to, get to the bottom of this. But not tonight. I'm going to bed."

"Well, if you can sleep after such a nightmare, fine. Just crawl back under the covers and act like nothing happened." Mollie sounded really angry now, but Hal didn't respond.

The next day they did give me a serious talking-to. I tried to explain about Mr. Murgrave and the Blue Hydrangea. I said I was sorry, that, yes, now I realized how dangerous it was to go sneaking around like that. No, I was not smoking cigarettes or marijuana. Yes, I understood that I was on restriction for six weeks, because this was really serious, and no, I would not hang around with Tim anymore.

I said the part about Tim just to make Mollie and Hal stop talking. I didn't really mean it.

Mollie blamed it all on Tim. She knew Evelyn and Edward, but Tim was a big question mark, and the fact that he lived over on Bogard Alley was enough of an answer for her. I knew it was useless to defend him, that it wouldn't do a bit of good to introduce Mollie to Tim's grandmother and her delicious biscuits.

In fact, I could not imagine, in my wildest dreams, either one of my parents walking up those dark stairs to Tim's apartment, or making conversation with Tim's mother when she came home from the hospital, or sitting in one of those rumpled chairs by the television in Tim's living room, which was also his dining room and his kitchen.

It was just one of those things that was never going to happen, not in a million years.

NINETEEN

I don't want you to get the wrong impression about Mollie. Or how I feel about Mollie. She is not as bad as I make her sound. To understand Mollie, you have to understand her mother.

Mollie once told me that she hated her mother from the time she was thirteen to the time she was thirty, when she had me. Only then did she begin to appreciate her mother. "When you have children," she says, "then you realize what your own mother went through."

Mollie's mother was a housewife who stayed home and cooked balanced meals and sewed matching outfits for the children. She made her own draperies and donated her time to charities. Her house was orderly, like a military ship, and she was faithful to her husband, even though he was mean and not faithful to her, because that was the way it was to be a good wife in those days, in the nineteen-fifties.

Of course Mollie hated her. Mollie was smart, she was beautiful, and she thought the only way to escape her mother was to hate her and everything about her: the suburban split-level house, the dark pink azaleas in careful rows, the manicured backyard with the pine straw raked up every day.

When Mollie had me she realized what it must have been like for her mother to raise three children without quite enough money, with a husband who came home at seven P.M. wanting his supper and his peace and quiet. Mollie realized how much *effort* her mother had put into being a mom.

Mollie isn't made out of the same sort of stuff. She doesn't enjoy suffering. Mollie probably would have been better off without a child, and it's a good thing she stopped when she did.

Mollie without a child would be able to move through the world unbound. I remember I once saw this movie about the dancer Isadora Duncan, who was so graceful that she walked on the earth as if it were made of foam rubber — floating really — until she got her scarf caught in the wheel of a motorcar and choked to death.

I think of myself as the scarf around Mollie's neck.

Mollie Unbound would be free. Beautiful without limits. Her life would be clutterless. No half-empty root beer bottles on the kitchen counter. No muddy sandals by the back door. No dirty towels on the bathroom floor. No divorce lawyers.

I love to think of her that way, without us. Perfect.

That is the way she was meant to be, and the rest is an accident she is dealing with the best she can.

TWENTY

I have been unlucky enough to grow up in the Age of Poison. Throughout history people have gotten freaked out about one danger or another, and the more they know the worse off they are. Which means that at this particular point in time the known dangers have just accumulated to the point where there is practically nothing you can do or eat without endangering your health.

Mollie reads the *New York Times* every day, and listens to the public radio station every morning when she wakes up. Monday through Saturday she gets the *Times* at the box in front of the post office, and on Sunday they reserve a copy for her at the bookstore. She isn't willing to wait until Monday for the local paper to reprint a big story about deadly gases leaking from heat pumps, for instance. They might not carry it after all, or they might leave out something important.

She knows everything there is to know about the radioactive garbage dripping into the water supply down near Savannah, the radon problem, the hole in the ozone layer. She knows the fat content of most foods, and goes crazy that Hal lets me eat French fries and hamburgers. Her latest worry is that she'll get cancer from high-voltage electric lines.

As far as I'm concerned, there is only one real threat to my health. I haven't heard about it on the radio and I doubt it's been reported in the *Times*, but I'm convinced it will kill me.

My alarm clock is dangerous to my health — those bright green numbers turning over and over all night long when I am trying to sleep, piercing holes in my eyelids. There is something definitely unnatural about them. Maybe they're radioactive. Maybe not. But they drive me nuts.

And my health is threatened every weekday by the little siren that goes off at six-thirty in the morning, the *beep, beep, beep* that won't stop until I reach out in the dark, blind, to hit the button on top of the green numbers.

One of these days we are going to read about alarm clocks, how we are poisoned nightly by the little green numbers pounding our exhausted brains, and how we are brutalized every morning, yanked out of our polluted sleep by the bedside siren.

This morning was worse than usual. The siren was set an hour early, for five-thirty. Henrietta Middleton has hired a lawyer for me, and the only time he could meet me was at six, at the coffee shop on Broad Street.

TWENTY-ONE

Henrietta met me at Hal's apartment and we rode down to The Cup together. She appeared at Hal's front door on a red Raleigh that was only a little bit too big for her. Henrietta seems to have quite an assortment of bicycles. "I bought it at the police sale. They didn't have anything exactly my size, but I'm still growing," she said, winking.

Actually, Henrietta is shrinking, and if she lives ten more years (which is unlikely, unless she stops running stoplights and entertaining criminals), she'll disappear completely. Mollie says she has some disease with a long name, osty-something, which comes from not drinking enough milk. Mollie thinks this is going to make me drink tons of milk. She forgets that shrinking is not one of my

91

big fears. I'd probably keep growing if I never ate another thing.

Anyway, Mrs. Middleton comes riding up on her red Raleigh with the sun rising right behind her — big hat, black shoes, funny clothes thrown together — a real apparition. I was glad it was early and none of the neighbors were up yet.

We got to The Coffee Cup in no time at all. Charleston has some traffic problems, but nothing like New York. This time of year you get tourists driving the wrong way down one-way streets, or going slow, just gawking at the beauty of the place. It's aggravating, but who can blame them?

The Coffee Cup, or The Cup, as the locals call it, is only a block from the courthouse, and most of the law offices are nearby. But the legal business going on at court and in those offices, says Mrs. Middleton, is merely a formality. The real work gets done at The Cup.

This is where you hear the latest legal gossip. Who is suing whom, who declared bankruptcy yesterday, who settled what case for a ton of money, who lost a motion in front of which judge. You never know when this kind of information is going to come in handy. For example, Henrietta says, if you're trying to settle your slip-and-fall case against the Price-Lo grocery story, it's essential to know that although Howard Waring got only two thousand for his last week, his client was an obnoxious exaggerator who seemed to slip and fall in grocery stores with some regularity.

At The Cup, also, you can try out your new legal theory on an eager audience. If it flies, you might include it in the brief you have to file with the Court of Appeals next week; if it falls flat, then you'll have to hit the books again.

The younger lawyers gather around the older stars. These are not necessarily the ones who've made the most money. The stars are all good lawyers who can try a case with the best of them, but they're also good storytellers. They can bring out the drama in the most ordinary case, like a reckless driving trial won yesterday in front of the magistrate. Who *wouldn't* drive off the road if a bumblebee flew in the window and landed on his nose? It doesn't matter that the fee was only a hundred and fifty dollars. It's the story that counts.

Henrietta says Drayton Guerard is the best of the storytellers, and the best lawyer in Charleston. He's related to her somehow, (as are at least half the city's inhabitants) and she was his high school English teacher. Maybe that's why he's agreed to represent me for free, but then again, it might be because he can spot a good story coming.

Henrietta is very persuasive, but she just doesn't have the stamina to deal with the likes of Walter Martin and Sonia Leonard, she says. Besides, she doesn't know the law; she only has common sense. "Common sense can be a real hindrance when you're dealing with the likes of Martin and Leonard," she says.

We are over in a corner of The Cup. Drayton Guerard is having his third cup of coffee. He is addicted to coffee, he says, but it beats a lot of other things he could be addicted to. "I used to be a drunk," he says, not even in a whisper, and as if he were already my best friend.

That Drayton Guerard was once a drunk is no secret, Henrietta told me later. He's proud that he's reformed and he goes to the A.A. meeting at the county library at least three times a week. A lot of his clients are A.A. beginners, people who come in still stinking of liquor, whose lives are broken into a hundred different pieces that Drayton Guerard will help put back together.

Drayton Guerard was once a drunk, and he's gone through two wives already, but now he's sober and it looks like the third wife will stick. She's a wonderful woman with a broad friendly face, she's a great cook, and she has the temperament to put up with Drayton's moodiness. She's so wholesome-looking, says Henrietta, that it's hard to imagine she was ever a drunk too, which she was. That's how they met, in A.A. Drayton says a Higher Power brought them together.

I am not at *all* sure about God and all that kind of thing. It sort of embarrasses me to talk about it. But Drayton will talk about the Higher Power at the drop of a hat. The Higher Power is patient, he says, and doesn't get upset with people who are not sure. The Higher Power doesn't have ego problems.

Henrietta says Drayton Guerard is the most brilliant student she ever had. Being a lawyer is probably a waste of his talents. He would have made a great writer. Or maybe a full-time wise man, like Mark Twain, if we still had those.

Drayton, like any good lawyer, gets the facts first. Henrietta tells the basic story, and I fill in what she leaves out. While we talk Drayton is slurping coffee and smacking on a blueberry muffin.

Drayton is sloppy, but not gross. His glasses need cleaning, and his blue seersucker suit is rumpled and maybe a size too small. His brain is too busy to be bothered with trifles like cleanliness and style. Even if he had the money, he wouldn't buy a huge new Mercedes with a car phone like some of the other lawyers. He lives downtown and usually walks to the office. His wife stays home. They have the groceries delivered. He despises travel. He is happy in Charleston and sees no need to go anywhere else.

Drayton wipes a drop of coffee off his lapel. "So," he says, looking at me, "what do *you* want to do about all this?"

"I want Mollie and Hal to get back together." This is not something I would tell just anybody, but since Drayton Guerard has been through so much himself I feel okay about it.

"Well, that's not something we have much control over. You have to hand that one over to the Higher Power. Let's assume they *don't* get back together. Then what? Where do you want to live?"

He has a way of asking a question so directly, you don't have to think long about how to answer it.

"I want to stay in my house. I don't want to go back and forth. It's my house as much as their house, whether they're in it together or not. It's my *home*. None of this stuff is my fault, so why should I be the one moving back and forth?"

"Good question," says Drayton, brushing blueberry muffin crumbs off the table. He looks at his watch — a cheap plastic one that you can buy at the drugstore. "Very good question. Ladies, I will work on it." Standing up, he leans a little toward us, almost but not quite bowing. He kisses Henrietta on the cheek and puts his hand on my shoulder.

I like the way this feels, the weight of his big hand, which is there only a second or two, but is steady and firm. I wonder if it has anything to do with the Higher Power, this feeling Drayton Guerard gives me with just a touch.

I like the feeling of being taken care of.

TWENTY-TWO

You remember Mary Rattick, the Rat. You might wonder why a woman would rat on her best friend, her college roommate, her jogging partner, why she would volunteer the business about the boyfriend cohabiting and all that.

It blew Mollie's mind when Hal walked out, even if he was only following instructions. She might have bounced back quicker, though, if it hadn't been for Mary Rattick ratting.

The fact of the matter was that Mary Rattick was telling the truth, and it wasn't the truth that was the problem, it was the *telling* that hurt.

I don't think Mollie would ask somebody to lie in court for her, but she would *want* them to lie without having to be asked. Especially her best friend. I mean, doesn't it sort of go without saying?

Not only did Mary not lie, she stuck herself right out there like that obnoxious Stephen Speigel who always knows the answer to every question and waves his skinny arm back and forth until the teachers have no choice but to call on him.

Mary gave the affidavit *reluctantly*, she said, and you could almost see the tears on the paper. She did it because it was the right thing to do, "for the child." She was "close friends" with "both parties to this controversy" and did not wish to "become antagonistic toward either," but "the mother is engaging in activity which is bound to be detrimental to this very sensitive and intelligent child." That's about all I remember from the paper in Judge Judge's office, but it's enough. I know baloney when I smell it, even in small quantities.

I figured the whole thing out sooner than Mollie did. Sometimes Mollie, who is an adult, cannot believe that adults actually behave as badly as they do. But who wants to believe her *best friend* is a traitor? Even in eighth grade we have a greater sense of loyalty.

The deal is that Mary the Rat has the hots for Hal. She's seen the Mollie *versus* Hal breakup coming for a long time. "It was inevitable," she says, "when the two of you were headed toward such different *places* in your lives." I have heard her say this to Mollie, and I can tell Mollie interprets it to mean that Mary thinks losing Hal is no great loss, he's been holding Mollie back, that it had to happen, and that both Mollie and Hal will be better off for the split.

I have also heard her say the same thing to Hal. She says it a lot more soothingly, and of course he takes it to mean that he's lucky to get off the fast track Mollie's running on, and that he's nobler because of it.

I have also watched Mary work her way up from patting Hal on the back to stroking the back of his head, to giving him a comforting peck on the cheek, and then a long heartfelt hug.

"You're so supportive," Hal says. "It's good to have real friends."

"I'm trying to stay neutral," says Mary. "We have a child to think about."

All of a sudden Mary and Hal have become "we." She's pretty subtle, this one. She knows the direct attack wouldn't work with Hal. And the child argument is a stroke of genius. He will do the right thing for "the child."

Soon she has him in bed, which, of course, I am

not supposed to know anything about because I went to sleep hours ago.

If Hal were not in love it might occur to him that he's doing exactly the same thing he's accused Mollie of, and that Mary the Rat is doing it with him.

Twenty-Three

I wonder how many important turns in life just happen without anybody thinking much about them, like when you're riding down a road and suddenly, there you are somewhere, even though you never made a conscious decision to get there at all.

After the Blue Hydrangea's arrest we never talked about disbanding. Sure, I knew that if Mollie caught me anywhere near the projects again I was probably going to be sent off to boarding school. But I didn't have to decide whether I was going to take a stand and defend Tim, or cave in and let Mollie have her way, because after the arrest Tim left town for a while.

Edward, Evelyn, and I managed to stay out of

Juvenile Court. Tim spent the weekend in the detention center, and no telling what would have happened to him in court if his father hadn't come down from Chicago and promised the judge he'd take Tim back with him. He'd give Tim a fresh start, he said. Maybe he was getting so big his grandmother couldn't control him anymore, he told the judge. Maybe a father's firm hand would help.

Without Tim, the Blue Hydrangea just lost all its energy. We were getting too old to be having a secret club, especially one whose main activity was going around leaving flower-messages on people's lawns and porches. Nobody actually *said* it, because we didn't have to, but before long, without anybody making a real decision, the Blue Hydrangea was no more.

And on top of that, Edward had to go and fall in love.

It started with the poetry. The summer after the Blue Hydrangea's arrest Mollie and Hal sent me off to camp for a month. It rained almost the whole time I was there, and the mountainside my cabin clung to turned into a big mudslide — red mud that wouldn't come out of my socks. Everything inside the cabin was damp. And my counselor was this prissy college girl who painted her nails all the time.

The aroma of mildew and nail polish almost drove me crazy. I probably have brain damage from the fumes.

So I was really glad when Edward's first letter came, even though it was a long boring one about how lonely he was and how much he wished I was around to cheer him up. He'd decided that life was basically meaningless, he wrote, and the only thing that mattered at all was poetry. He'd decided he'd become a poet. It would be a great sacrifice. He'd have to give up everything — money, a normal life — but it would be worth it.

The first poems were about meaninglessness and boredom, which made them pretty meaningless and boring:

> *I came from the void*
> *and I will go to the void.*
> *My life stretches out*
> *in front of me like a*
> *long dark road.*

That was it. What was I supposed to say? Edward sounded really depressed, but I couldn't write back, "You sound really depressed." Instead I wrote, "Your poem is great. You have a lot of talent. I miss you. Love, Mac." It was a lie that I thought the poem was great, but what harm would it do? And I really did miss Edward in a funny kind of way.

The next week, when the river rose almost to the edge of the camp and all outdoor activities had to be canceled, I got a thick envelope from Edward. I couldn't possibly read all this stuff, but a few of the poems grabbed my attention:

Her eyes are like stars
shining in my dark sky.
Her hair is my blanket
against the cold winter . . .

And so on. Was Edward in love? Like a dummy, in my next letter I just asked him: "Are you in love with somebody?"

Looking back on it, I can't believe I was that stupid. He didn't have time to answer before I left for home, but when Mollie and Hal picked me up the first thing out of Hal's mouth was, "Edward Heinz has been calling to find out when you're getting back. He says he wants to take you to a movie." Hal winked, as if he and I shared some big secret.

All of a sudden it hit me. Edward is in love with *me*.

It was horrifying. Out of the question. I wasn't

ready to be in love with anybody, and certainly not Edward. Edward had been my friend for so long I couldn't imagine him being anything else.

Then I made another mistake. I told Evelyn. More about that later. . .

TWENTY-FOUR

Harvey is getting better at talking to me. Or maybe I am getting better at talking to Harvey. I really do like having her to talk to, once a week.

At this point, there are only three people I can tell the truth to: Henrietta, Harvey, and Drayton Guerard. Actually, when you think about it, I am better off in the truth department than I was before Hal and Mollie decided to get a divorce. Then I couldn't really talk to anybody. The Blue Hydrangea Society was defunct, and I was alone.

I made a deal with Harvey after a couple of sessions. I would answer her questions if she would answer some of mine.

She was really quiet after I proposed this deal. She knew it was a test. Then she said, "You know,

Mac, your parents are paying me to help you talk about this whole situation. It's my job to help you think about *your* life, not to talk about *mine*."

"That might be," I answered, "but if I won't talk to you unless you talk to me, then you can't do your job."

"Okay," she said. So I get to ask one question of Harvey for each three questions she asks me.

I like to ask questions. I like to interview people. When Mollie and Hal used to have parties and strangers came over, my favorite thing was to interrogate them right after they'd had their first glass of wine. I didn't let them off the hook until they'd given me all the essential information — how they got to Charleston, what they did for a living, whether they were married, had children, etc., what they liked and didn't like, and so forth. I usually got most of the information I needed in about three minutes.

This is what I found out about Harvey:

She grew up in New York City, but not the good part. Her father drank a lot and yelled all the time about things that were out of his control, which was almost everything. He owned an automobile repair shop and was barely making a go of it when the city condemned his property to build an overpass. He was temporarily rich, but after he got the check he realized his whole life had been a mistake because he had thought that money would bring happiness, and here he had more money than he'd ever had before and he was still miserable. This realization sent him over the edge, literally, because he then jumped off the overpass onto the concrete, leaving his wife, Harvey, and three other children.

Harvey was smart and used her share of the money to go to college and graduate school. She decided she would try to learn about what makes people happy and what makes people unhappy. She wanted to keep people from jumping off bridges. She became a psychiatrist.

I asked her if she was happy.

"It depends," she said. "It depends on what aspect of my life you're talking about."

I had never really thought about dissecting happiness, you know, dividing it up into little pieces like a frog in biology lab. I mean, it seems to me you are either happy or you are unhappy.

But Harvey explained that as people get older they get more complicated, and they sometimes think about their lives as not one whole thing, but as lots of pieces pulled together. You're not a total failure, she says. You're never a total success. You're good at some things and not others. You may be satisfied with some parts of your life and dissatisfied with others.

So I ask her to tell me what she is good at.

"Cooking," she says. She cooks great lentil soup. She wishes she had somebody to cook for. Also gardening, because she grew up surrounded by concrete. She especially treasures her little plot of earth down on Tradd Street. She grows enormous flowers like foxgloves and hollyhocks, and beds of snapdragons so yellow you could eat your heart out. Sometimes she sits at the back of the garden, right on the ground, and just smells the wetness of the dirt.

I ask her if she thinks her flowers are a substitute for children. It is my turn to play psychiatrist now.

Perhaps so, she says. She likes taking care of them and watching them grow. When she says this her voice is not as smooth as usual.

I think for a minute I would like to reach out and touch Harvey's hand, but I'm afraid it might make her cry.

It's her turn. She asks me to think about myself as a grownup, old enough to be beyond all this, with my own life, with a husband if I want one, with my own children. She asks me to take all I've learned and make it part of my life, to use it wisely.

I tell her I don't think I'll get married. Maybe I'll adopt some children. Maybe I'll just live alone, which would be a lot less complicated.

TWENTY-FIVE

Looking back on what happened between me and Edward, I think it wouldn't have been so awful if Evelyn hadn't interfered.

I think I would have told him how I honestly felt, maybe not right away, but soon enough. I would have told him I wasn't ready to be in love with anybody. I wouldn't have let things get so out of control.

But I made the mistake of telling Evelyn all about the poems.

I told her how panicked I was, how I just wanted to clear things up with Edward right away, to get us back to just being friends.

"You're such an *idiot*," she said. "He's a pretty nice guy. Maybe not what you want in the long run. But so what? You have to start somewhere."

This was just like Evelyn. Was love like some sort of science project you planned out and worked on until you got the snazzy display that you wanted? But I didn't say this to Evelyn, because she *did* seem to know more about these things than I did. She'd had a lot more experience. She'd already been through two steady boyfriends and was on number three, a guy from Middleton High who had his own car and played on the football team.

It was amazing, really, how Evelyn could accomplish so much in just a couple of years. She made me feel backward, like my whole life was a social hand-me-down.

But I let Evelyn convince me to let the Edward thing "run its course." That was the exact phrase she used. It sounded like what the doctor says when you go in with a virus. "I'm afraid it's just going to have to run its course."

The theory, according to Evelyn, was that having a boyfriend, even if it was only Edward, would make other guys notice me more. This seemed very logical. It's just that I never asked myself if I really cared whether other guys noticed me more.

The next thing I knew, I was at the movies with Edward. Sure, we had been to the movies before, but not like this. Edward had ruined everything by sending me those poems. Now every little thing he did made me nervous.

I can't even remember what the movie was, because the minute the lights went out and the previews started I was totally miserable. Edward must have been miserable, too. He is just incapable of being cool, and when he swung his arm over my shoulders it felt like he'd hit me with a brick. I held on to my popcorn so hard that I squeezed the shape out of the cardboard, and popcorn started spilling out all over the place, which at least gave me an excuse to lean down.

I hoped that by the time I sat up, his arm wouldn't be on the back of my seat. But after a few more minutes *there it was again*, on my shoulders, heavy and hot.

I felt nauseated. "I think I'm going to throw up," I said, and I bolted for the restroom. I stayed there a long time, probably half an hour at least, and when I came out the movie was over and Edward was standing by the video game machine, looking pathetic.

"Are you okay?" he asked, and I mumbled something about coming down with a cold, but it wasn't very convincing.

We didn't say a word on the way back downtown. His father drove us home. I wasn't going to take any more chances. I sat in the front seat next to Edward's father and that left Edward in the back seat all by himself. I was glad I didn't have to look at him. When they dropped me off at my house I jumped out of the car, barely saying thank-you, and ran upstairs.

I dialed Evelyn's number. I didn't care if it *was* after ten P.M. and her mother was going to have a fit. Evelyn answered.

I wasn't crying, but almost. I felt my whole body about to explode. "I hate you, Evelyn. I hate you so much. Just do me a favor and don't ever speak to me again."

When I hung up I couldn't believe I had finally said it.

Now Tim was gone, I had insulted Edward, and Evelyn would probably never speak to me again.

I was alone, and most of it was my own doing.

TWENTY-SIX

I'm not the first kid Henrietta has been Guardian over. She tells me about them. There was Willard who lived up near the air base, whose father beat him and broke his arm. The police took Willard away and when his mother went to court to get him back, the judge told her she could have him, but she'd have to leave her husband. She did, but not for long, and when she went back home he beat Willard up again and almost killed him. So Henrietta had no choice but to recommend that Willard be sent away to a foster home. She writes him postcards, rides the bus to Lancaster every couple of weeks to see him, and about once a month she sends him a tin of chocolate chip cookies.

It's been a long time now since Willard's mother

visited him, and even longer since his father paid any support, so Henrietta says Willard will be free for adoption in a couple of months. The only problem is, Willard is nine years old, large for his age, and there is nothing cute about him. He stutters and has trouble in school. He likes to start fires. It will be hard to find a family crazy enough to take Willard but strong enough to deal with him.

She tells me about others: Annie, the baby who got left in a dumpster; Mendel, the teenage boy who earned his allowance picking up women for his father; Alice, who was about my age and from a nice family but whose mother had to go into the mental hospital when her father ran off with another woman. And on and on.

It begins to occur to me that I, Henrietta Middleton's current assignment, am not such a big problem after all. I am your average, screwed-up kid from an above-average, screwed-up family; but nobody is beating me, leaving me in a dumpster, sexually abusing me, or sending me off to a foster home.

I ask Henrietta how she copes with all these hopeless cases. She says she doesn't have any magic solutions, she just has fortitude. I like the way she says "fortitude," emphasizing the *t*'s. She will not let things wear her down. She will not take no for an answer. She will keep on talking and working, and if all else fails, she will just hold a child's hand and help him get through a bad day.

Sometimes it is not enough. Sometimes it makes a difference.

"When I go to bed at night," Henrietta says, "I know I am *somebody*."

I wonder where Henrietta got her toughness, her sense of sureness about who she is and what she is doing in this world. I would like to pinch off a piece of it. I tell her how I feel, dizzy and rootless, as though I am about to fall off something.

She smiles and sips her sherry. She tells me about Dr. Middleton and how she fell in love with him, how they bought this old house and lived in it and raised their children, how she read to him after he had his stroke and went blind, and why she is determined to stay here even though the children are all grown up with children of their own and the place is much too big for her, a "regular main-tenance nightmare."

She knows where she belongs. Not just in the physical sense, not just in this funky old house in this borderline neighborhood in this town tilting on the edge of the ocean. She is connected to her past, her memories, and she is making her connections every day with kids like Willard, Annie, and me.

Henrietta is like my fig tree. She will endure.

I tell her I wish I could be so strong.

"You are," she says. "You are stronger than you think."

And maybe I believe her.

TWENTY-SEVEN

Sonia Leonard and Walter Martin are getting really fired up now. They have swapped lists of witnesses. It seems everybody who's ever said so much as "hello" to Mollie, Hal, or me is going to be testifying. All our neighbors, my pediatrician, my ballet teacher, the members of Mollie's book club, Hal's fraternity brothers, Mary Rattick, Michael McMenamin, Mollie's psychiatrist, Hal's psychiatrist. They've put Harvey on the list, too, but Drayton Guerard says they can go to hell, and I'm not to worry about it.

In the last couple of days Martin and Leonard have bombarded my school, sending their people in to interview my teachers, the principal, the assistant principal, the guidance counselor, and even Mrs. Matthews, the librarian. It's very embarrassing.

My classmates are beginning to think I must have some terrible problem.

It seems that where I go to school is a big issue. If Mollie gets custody, says Hal, I'll be going to Rutledge Prep. Rutledge Prep is okay, he says, but it's mostly a social statement, and it won't meet my "educational, intellectual, and creative needs." Mollie is agitated because if Hal gets to choose, he'll put me in the public high school for gifted children. They have a great art and theater program, which is what I'm really into, but Mollie worries about the social atmosphere: kids there are bused in from all over the county, some from really raunchy neighborhoods, and the school itself sits in the middle of a bad neighborhood.

Of course, as usual, neither Hal nor Mollie has asked me what I think.

If they asked me, I'd tell them I doubt it makes a whole lot of difference whether I go to Rutledge Prep or the public high school. They both have nice buildings and good teachers. What they *don't* have, from what I've heard, is any imagination. The teachers may be really brilliant, but their talents are wasted because of the stupid rules they have to put up with.

Maybe when I grow up I'll run my own school.

Most of the time, *my* students won't be behind

their desks; they'll be out in the city exploring. Why should I keep them in a boring brick box all day long scribbling in workbooks and copying things off a blackboard? If I weren't cooped up in school, I could do some of the things I've always wanted to do, like go over to the docks and watch the giant machines lift the containers off the container ships. I'd like to find out where the ships come from, how long it took them to get here, where the bananas (or whatever is in those containers) were grown, and what kind of people grew them.

I'd like to spend a day or two digging under one of the old buildings downtown with the archaeologists from the university.

I'd like to go out on the shrimp boats from Shem Creek, out past the jetties and into the ocean. I've never been out there. I'd like to watch the shrimp nets drop down to the sea, and see what comes up in them.

At *my* school we'd write our own plays and produce them every semester. We would read all the great old stuff to get ideas: Shakespeare and Tennessee Williams. We'd learn how to use a sewing machine and make our own costumes.

If I could design my own school, I'd never want to graduate.

TWENTY-EIGHT

I have been thinking a lot about the Higher Power.

Before I met Drayton Guerard, I was not concerned at all about God and that sort of thing. Mollie and Hal don't go to church. Mollie seems to think if you go to church you can't be too bright.

Hal once took me to the Baptist Sunday School because he had grown up Baptist and it seemed the right sort of thing to do. Mollie almost had a fit when I came home singing Baptist songs and talking about hell. She made Hal swear he wouldn't take me back. Needless to say, Walter Martin will bring this up at the trial.

I am not the sort of person who is likely to go for an idea like the Higher Power. Or at least not until lately.

123

Before Mollie and Hal split up, I sometimes thought of my life as just a series of arrangements, as if all I needed to make a success of it was a calendar and enough ballpoint pens and name tags. I thought if you were organized and planned well enough, everything would work out.

When Mollie and Hal and I were all together, the surface of our days was cool and smooth, and even though things weren't perfect, all the complicated stuff stayed inside and out of sight. When they split up, it was like an egg cracking. Now there is this amazing mess that nobody wants to clean up.

Once this kind of thing happens it occurs to you maybe there is more to the world than eggs breaking without any reason. Things break, bad things happen, and people die, even though they have been careful and well-organized. Maybe it's wishful thinking, but you begin to hope somebody is in charge.

There was only one other time in my life when I thought about God, although I didn't know it at the time. I was about five, and standing in the flower bed between the sidewalk and the street. It was October — chilly, but not cold enough to go inside. The sun lit the edges of things like fire.

No other people were in sight. I remember thinking, for the first time, that one day my life would come to an end. I didn't feel any sadness, but this very small and sharp awareness, like a pain that would grow.

At that moment, when I realized I would not be here forever, I also had this very intense feeling of comfort. It is hard to describe. I became connected to things, not just a kid playing on the curb, but a part of the street, the neighborhood, the world, and the universe. I could step back and watch myself playing, and I felt more than five years old. I felt part of something enormous, and even if I had to die, which was terrifying, I would not entirely disappear.

I talked to Henrietta about it one afternoon outside the museum. She had invited me to take a walk downtown so that we could discuss the trial, which would be coming up soon, but we ended up talking about God.

Henrietta says she believes in God, but not the God most people believe in. She says that her God is not some old man sitting up in heaven issuing directives and deciding the fate of the world, but a spirit moving in the hearts of human beings, the force of love that endures despite all odds. When she prays, she says, she listens to the voice of this spirit in her own heart, and sometimes she can really hear it, even above the noise and traffic of life.

She does not believe in hell, except the hell

human beings make for each other because they are stupid and selfish. As for life after death, she thinks it is silly to say that individual people live on into eternity, but it makes sense to her that love is eternal, that it is passed on from generation to generation, and that is enough for her.

As for churches, she says, they are fine. But holy places are everywhere, if we will just find them.

We found one that afternoon. This place has been there all along, and I have walked past it a thousand times without noticing. We turned off King Street, where the gateway opened onto the path that cut through the middle of the block.

It was an ordinary old gate, in need of painting, nothing remarkable for my town, but it led into another world. Not a street, or even an alley, just a brick path through the middle of the city. On either side were the back doors of apartments, small gardens with statues, private places. Farther on, the path opened into a graveyard where the gravestones were so old you could hardly read the names on them. Flowers were everywhere, in no particular order, wild ones of almost every color, and yellow roses climbing the stones. It was too bad the Blue Hydrangea Society was defunct.

"If you die, you should be buried here." I said this

to Henrietta without even thinking, and then it occurred to me she might be offended.

Instead, she smiled. "I'm not quite ready for that yet. Someone has to make sure Drayton Guerard is doing his job."

TWENTY-NINE

We are two weeks away from trial and Harvey has a crisis.

It is not good when your therapist has a crisis. They are not supposed to do that. But because Harvey and I have this deal that I can ask *her* questions, too, I have found out a lot more than most people do about their therapists.

I have found out, for instance, that Harvey is not happy about going to court.

She is worried that whatever she says will be misinterpreted, twisted into something she doesn't really mean, and that she will not be smart enough to tell the Judge what he needs to hear. She is shy, she says. She became a psychiatrist because she wanted to help people work through their problems, but privately, and not on a stage.

Harvey is so shy, she says, that when she thinks about testifying in front of the Judge, Mollie, Hal, Sonia Leonard, Walter Martin, a court reporter, a deputy sheriff, and Henrietta, she starts to sweat. This is irrational, she says, and perhaps she should talk to her therapist about it.

This makes me laugh, which feels good, and we both laugh. The thought of Harvey having a therapist is positively delicious. Even Harvey can see that. Nevertheless, she remains very serious about the hard job ahead of her. She puts a straight index finger to her lips. "Be quiet a minute," she says, "I've got to think."

The crisis is that Sonia Leonard has told Walter Martin she is going to subpoena Harvey's records, the tests I took and my tapes — everything I have told Harvey since Day One.

She should have known, she says, that it was coming. This is standard procedure in a case like this.

I think it is sometimes helpful to think about complicated things in the simplest way possible, and to try to figure out what feels right and what feels wrong.

So I say, "This isn't just a case. You and I are

friends now. And friends shouldn't have their private conversations exposed in court."

I have an idea.

"Harvey, if I tell you to destroy all my records, destroy the tapes, can you do that?"

"Of course not," she answers.

"I didn't think so. And anyway, I might want some of this stuff later. So, I will ask you, please, to turn these things over to my Guardian *ad litem*, Henrietta Porter LePage Middleton, for safekeeping. She will take good care of them."

Harvey was about to protest, although I could tell she didn't really know why she should, when I said, in the most forceful way possible, "I *instruct* you to turn these records over to Henrietta Middleton. Immediately. They belong to *me*."

I sounded like my parents when they say, "I really *mean* it, Mac." And I did.

THIRTY

I wasn't supposed to, but I found out what Mollie said when Drayton Guerard asked her how she would "do" him over.

"Let's just suppose," he said, "that my law firm contracted with you to redo my image. Where would you start?"

"First, Mr. Guerard, I would want to make sure your firm understands the importance of *whole* environment design. It won't do much good to do just one lawyer. I offer a better rate for the whole firm, including the support staff. I also *insist* on rehabilitating the interior, but I give a discount on this, depending on the size of the firm."

"Interior?" Drayton asked.

"Furniture, carpeting, et cetera. Appropriate small art objects and paintings. All very tasteful."

"Oh," he said, "I thought you might be talking about my soul. That" — and here the court reporter indicated there was a pause — "is probably beyond rehabilitation."

This priceless stuff is preserved forever in a hundred and twenty double-spaced pages bound in clear plastic and entitled, "Henry Howard Whitford, Plaintiff, *versus* Margaret Garrett Whitford, Defendant, In the Family Court of the Ninth Judicial Circuit, Case No. 92 – 5320."

Walter Martin sent Hal a copy and Hal left it on his bedside table. My father has marked it up with red-penciled comments like "Untrue," "a gross exaggeration," and "I vehemently deny it."

This little booklet of conversation between Drayton and Mollie is something called a deposition. When I asked Drayton about it, he said lawyers invented depositions when they got tired of unpleasant surprises at trial. Sometimes, he says, the lawyers take so many depositions they have to be hauled around in suitcases. What was supposed to make things simpler has made them more complicated.

In the case of Hal *versus* Mollie there have already been thirteen depositions. Drayton says most divorce cases don't have this many, but my mom and dad have paid their lawyers a lot of money and the lawyers had better have something to show for it.

Mollie wasn't the least bit reluctant to tell Drayton what she could do to improve him. "First, I think it would be helpful to improve your color, Mr. Guerard. This can be accomplished with some of the new tanning creams, which will give you a bronze look while sparing you any unnecessary exposure to the sun, which at your age can be very dangerous. Next, I'd set you up with my nutritionist for the low-fat diet. I understand you cut out alcohol several years ago, but perhaps you do not yet realize the need for other major changes in your consumption patterns."

This was as close as Mollie was going to come to saying, "You're a pale-skinned, fat old man." Drayton Guerard egged her on.

"Mrs. — uh — Whitford, I *do* realize the need for these changes, it's just that, as Mark Twain said, when they tell you your ship is sinking you'd better have something left to throw overboard. Gluttony is my only remaining sin, and I am saving it for a rainy day. As for the tanning lotion, I have conducted my entire career as a white man, and it might be very confusing to my wife, my ex-wives, my children, and my clients if I were to suddenly turn brown.

Perhaps you have some other suggestions." (Of course the court reporter did not write down that Drayton Guerard was looking smug, but I'm sure he must have been.)

"I object," said Sonia Leonard. "That's not even a question, and besides, it's not at all relevant."

"On the contrary," said my lawyer, "I believe Mrs. Whitford's beliefs about how to reform human beings are of the utmost importance in this custody case. After all, should she become the custodial parent she will certainly have an unlimited opportunity to practice what she preaches."

So Drayton went on, and Mollie fell into the trap, despite her lawyer's warning. I imagined Sonia must have been kicking her under the table about now, but Mollie simply cannot resist the opportunity to redesign people, and just to *talk* about redesigning them is almost as good.

She told Drayton that he would have to throw away all his old clothes, especially his rumpled seersucker suit with the yellow stains on it (she was kinder than that in her description of it, but he got the point) and the white buck shoes that weren't quite white anymore. She gave him the names of a couple of shops where he might buy his new wardrobe, all of them sounding expensive. She suggested that he enroll in a yoga class to improve his posture. Lastly, she said, she recommended that he consider a speech therapist so that he could get rid of his heavy accent.

"Accent? I didn't know I had an accent."

"Oh, yes," Mollie said. "It's easy to place it. Old Charleston with New England education, very difficult for strangers to understand. It's almost like a foreign language."

"I don't talk to strangers very often, Ms. Whitford. If they can't understand me, they can go back where they came from."

"Objection!" said Sonia Leonard. "We are not going to waste my client's good money listening to your philosophy of life, Mr. Guerard."

"I should think that might be one of the *better* uses of your client's good money, Sonia," Drayton fired back.

Drayton Guerard went on to ask my mother more about how she would redesign him, how she would redesign her husband, and even how she would redesign me. I don't know whether I was afraid to read this last part, or what, but sitting on Hal's bed reading this stuff I got so sleepy I could hardly keep my eyes open.

I put the deposition back where I'd found it and pulled Hal's pillow over my head until I fell asleep.

THIRTY-ONE

Henrietta and I are in New York City, at the Plaza Hotel. The trial starts in a couple of days, and Hal and Mollie are in a total frenzy. They don't even speak to each other when they exchange me anymore. They pass notes back and forth to each other instead.

"Mac has a social studies test tomorrow. Please review the products of Ecuador, Colombia, and Peru with her. She seems a little weak on these." This from Mollie.

"Mac has a rash on her neck. She says she thinks she may be allergic to spinach. Could you check this out with Dr. Arthur?" This one from Hal, who is sometimes really gullible.

Anyway, you might wonder why Henrietta and I are at the Plaza.

It turns out that before the separation Hal bought tickets for me and Mollie to spend Mother's Day in the Big Apple together, but after Hal filed for divorce Walter Martin told him it wasn't such a great idea for me to be spending time with my mother in my favorite place, so he threatened to cancel the reservations unless he could take me himself. Sonia Leonard had a fit, and made a motion for the Judge to decide what to do with the airline tickets and the room at the Plaza. The Judge called in Drayton Guerard, who suggested — it was really brilliant — that Henrietta take me. I would get back in time to have supper with Mollie on Mother's Day, he told the Judge, and the weekend in New York would give me a much-needed break from the tense relationship between my parents.

I definitely have the best lawyer in Charleston. And so here we are.

I think maybe this is another turning point in my life. I still talk on the tapes for Harvey, but now I have my own diary too. I write for myself. I went to the bookstore and bought one of those books with blank pages. The cover is cloth and the edges of the paper look like swirls of raspberry sauce in vanilla ice cream. I have only filled in a couple of pages, and when I look at all the blank pages left to write in I feel like my life is just beginning.

New York City is a good place to begin your life over again. Sometimes it will leave you alone, let your feel totally anonymous, as if you are just an inconsequential speck in the universe. Other times it will come right up to you and hug you, pressing you with its people and not letting go. When you are ready to begin your life over again you can come here and sit in a crowd and find somebody who looks just like the kind of person you'd like to become. You might strike up a conversation with this person on the Staten Island Ferry. You might fall in love with this person. This person may know somebody you knew a long time ago and forgot about until now. Or this person may say something really mysterious and intelligent which you will never forget.

It's like that in New York City.

The possibilities are endless. I have heard people say you can't really *live* there, and maybe that is true, but at least you can get an inspiration about *how* to live, and then you can go back home to wherever you are from and you will be more interesting.

To be in New York City with someone like

Henrietta Middleton is to increase the possibilities a million times. Even in Charleston, she attracts interesting people like a magnet. But here in New York she is sensational.

We have tea in the Palm Court at the Plaza. "Just like Eloise," she says, and when I ask her who Eloise is, she grabs me by the hand and takes me down the hall to see the huge portrait of the spunky kid who lived in the Plaza with her mother. Eloise is as real as you can be and still be only a character in a book. Her mother is a lot like Mollie, but she spends most of her time in Miami. Eloise could have been just a lonely, nerdy little kid, but she had style, and she made a name for herself at the Plaza.

I want to be like that, to make people notice me. Not because I am obnoxious, but because I am interesting.

In New York City you learn that there is a very fine line between being interesting and being obnoxious. This is especially true if you ride the subway. If we ever have a nuclear war, and the only people left are the ones on the subway, the future of the human race will be changed forever.

Hal and Mollie would have a total fit if they knew Henrietta and I were riding the subway. They think only murderers and perverts ride the subway. Not true. There are definitely some perverts, and probably a few murderers, but most of the passengers are just people who do nothing but look intense.

This is especially true around the Washington Square stop. Have you ever noticed that? They look as if they are posing for one of those modern photographs in coffee table books. They wear a lot of black, and jewelry that looks like prison chains. Maybe it's just because Henrietta is with me, and she is a strangeness magnet. Or maybe it's like this all the time.

We get out at New York University. This is where I think I'll go to college, probably over my parents' dead bodies. We walk to Chinatown. The streets are packed with people going about their business, and lined with stalls of strange vegetables I have never seen before. Musky smells spill out of the doorways. We go into a dark restaurant and I feel foreign — everybody else is Chinese. Henrietta is oblivious. If she were in Beijing she wouldn't feel uncomfortable or out of place, so why should she here?

We take a cab back to the Plaza. The cabby is from some exotic place with an unpronounceable name. His skin is grayish brown and his eyes are huge and black. He speaks only a little English, but elegantly. How he manages to be elegant in this dumpy cab bumping up Sixth Avenue toward the Plaza, I don't know. I'm too tired to interview him.

I fall asleep on Henrietta's shoulder, and only when she has gotten me into my nightgown and tucked the wonderful crisp sheets around my shoulders does she tell me that the cabby has royal blood, there is a revolution going on in his native country, and he has barely escaped, leaving his fiancée behind. He is earning money to send to her so that she can join him in this country. They will marry and live here and have children. The children will be princes and princesses, and one day perhaps they will go back to the old country and claim their rightful places. In the meantime, he says, he will be content for them to be Americans.

This kind of story is more likely to be true in a place like New York. Nevertheless, as I am falling to sleep, it occurs to me that maybe Henrietta has made it up to entertain me. Or maybe to entertain herself. Whatever, it is inspirational. It's about true love, and no matter how unlikely it may be that true love really exists I want to believe in it.

THIRTY-TWO

Our plane was late taking off from New York, so it was dark by the time we got back to Charleston. Maybe that's what threw me off. I got my weeks mixed up, forgot about Mother's Day and thought I was supposed to be with Hal, so when the taxi deposited me at his apartment I was surprised that nobody came to the door. I went around to the back, where he keeps a key for me under a flower pot, and went in through the kitchen.

I was quiet, because it was so late, and Hal was probably asleep already.

I groped my way through the kitchen, down the hall, and was about to go into my bedroom and turn on the light when I heard them talking.

Hal wasn't asleep, but he was in bed. With the Rat.

I am not ordinarily a sneaky person, but what was I supposed to do? Announce myself? Say something dumb, like "Hi, guys. How *are* you? I had a great time in New York." Or "Excuse me, I didn't mean to interfere." Or maybe I could have just gone to bed and waked up in the morning as if nothing was weird, chewed my cereal over Hal's flea market breakfast table and gone off to school without a word about the fact that my father was in bed with my mother's (former) best friend.

Instead, I leaned against the door frame and listened, trying not to breathe too loud.

"You've got to get more aggressive, honey," said the Rat. Then there were some sounds which I interpreted as smooching. "You've got to stand up for yourself. If you don't, we're going to lose Mac. Do you want her to grow up with that screwed-up sense of values? She's your only kid, Hal."

My father made romantic noises that were almost words but not quite. I could hear the mattress squeaking underneath them.

"Let's not talk about it *now*," Hal said.

All of a sudden the bedside lamp was on and I had to step back so they wouldn't see me standing there at the door, my eyes blinking. The Rat sat up in bed, not looking at all romantic.

"This is silly," she said, pulling on her underwear. "You need your sleep. Tomorrow is a big day."

My father reached past the Rat and turned the light off. The mattress creaked. Quiet for a minute, then more kissing sounds.

The Rat: "I can't respect somebody who won't even . . ."

Hal: "I'm doing everything Walter tells me to do. He seems to be doing a pretty good job."

The Rat: "He told you to get the tapes and you won't do it."

Hal: "The shrink doesn't have them anymore. She says she turned them over to Henrietta Middleton, at Mac's request. What do you want me to do, go after the old lady? If she has the tapes, she probably doesn't even remember where she put them. And besides which, who wants to listen to a thirteen-year-old talking to herself?"

The Rat: "You're going to find out what she's really thinking. And right now, I'd guess she's pretty down on her mother. She knows about Michael McMenamin, and I don't think she likes it a bit. Also, I'll bet Mac can see through Mollie. The kid has a lot of common sense. It's amazing, with a mother like that."

144

This made me want to turn on the light, throw the Rat out, and defend my mother. Mollie is a mess right now, but she's not *totally* without redeeming qualities.

"Okay," Hal said, not moaning anymore, but sounding desperate. "You're right. I'll do it. I'll unleash Walter and he can do whatever he has to do to get the tapes. Maybe we'll just have to send the sheriff after Henrietta Middleton."

And that was all it took to make Mary Rattick the most amorous rat in the world. I didn't announce myself until they were finished. I went back out to the kitchen, slammed the back door loud enough to cause an earthquake. Hal came running out in his bathrobe.

"You're supposed to be at your mother's. I *know* you'd rather be here, honey, but we have to play by the rules." Naturally Hal thought I did this on purpose. "Why don't you give her a call and tell her I'll run you over there first thing in the morning?"

I knew the Rat would be waiting until I fell asleep to sneak out of my father's apartment. I knew they would be lying there in his bed whispering about me, and Mary would probably be attributing some deep psychological meaning to my coming to my father's house so soon before the trial.

The truth is, I forget where I'm supposed to be. I

don't want to be in this apartment with my lovelorn father any more than I want to be in Mollie's house for a week of spinach and asparagus and my mother missing Michael McMenamin.

I just want to be home, the way it used to be, even if it wasn't perfect.

Or if that won't work out, maybe I could just ride the subway in New York City all day long, meeting fascinating people and having interesting conversations, eating Chinese food and wearing heavy jewelry. I would be pale. I would wear dark red lipstick and white powder that would make me look sort of sick, in an interesting way.

I would see all the latest openings at the galleries in SoHo. I would memorize every line from *Phantom of the Opera*. I would know the subway map like the back of my hand.

The whole city would adopt me, everybody would know me, people would clap when I come up out of the subway into the shining streets, and even perverts and murderers would be respectful.

THIRTY-THREE

I called Mollie last night, and explained that I was sorry I was not where I was supposed to be.

She was mad. Of course she thought I'd done it on purpose.

Hal was mad, too. He acted as if he was pleased to have me, but I could tell he was really irritated.

He dropped me off about a block from Mollie's so I could get my books and she could take me to school. He won't go anywhere near her house anymore. "*I* try to avoid confrontations," he says, meaning, of course, that he is not ever the one who starts the trouble, and that if there is a problem it is all her doing.

I didn't go to Mollie's. I didn't get my books. I didn't go to school.

I remembered Hal's conversation with the Rat. I'd been half asleep, but not too far gone to pick up on the gist of it.

Maybe, I thought, it isn't too late to get to Henrietta's before the sheriff does.

It was raining hard. Every two or three weeks, this time of year, we have one of these downpours. Water doesn't just fall, it *shoots* out of the sky, as if Charleston were some kind of target. We go under. The streets near the rivers fill up enough to row a canoe through them. Traffic comes to a halt. Roofs, even the new ones, leak.

Today is worse than usual for May. Ashley Avenue above Montagu Street is totally flooded. Windshield wipers wave back and forth in a desperate sort of dance, and frustrated drivers honk their horns as if it makes a difference.

I have an advantage on my bicycle. I imagine the sheriff's car coming to a stop at the corner of East Bay and Calhoun, its blue light turning frantically, the water swooshing up over the hood and into the engine. He will have to walk to Henrietta Middleton's house.

Charlotte Street, her street, is on high ground. People are leaving for work. Children in their shiny yellow raincoats come out of houses into the dark morning.

The big iron gate is swinging open in the wind. Maybe the sheriff has beat me here after all. What is left of Henrietta's spring garden leans sideways, pummelled by the heavy rain. She has taught me the names of these flowers: snapdragons, daisies, dianthus. I make a mental note to talk to Frank, the current resident ex-con. The garden needs attention.

I ring the bell. Maybe she can't hear with the rain pounding her tin roof. I ring it again. Where is Frank? He doesn't have a job. He should be here, even if Henrietta has gone to the museum early.

The porch door is half open. I will talk to her about being more careful. Yes, I will say, people are mostly good, but now and then somebody will come along who isn't so good, and you need to start being more careful. The world is changing.

The first thing I notice is that the silver is gone, those huge pieces that used to sit on the sideboard, the kind of stuff most people keep locked up in cabinets and only bring out for special occasions. But Henrietta keeps it out all the time, gloriously polished and the only thing shiny in this house that is falling down around her.

The stairs creak under my feet, winding round and round to the second floor. The wood is worn almost white, the banister about to come loose. I'll ask Frank about this, too. Maybe he knows how to fix things.

The rain is coming down harder now. I can hear it popping against the tin roof. It is not a question of *whether* there will be leaks, but *where*. I remember Henrietta once told me she had a dream about roofers. She dreamed the whole world had nothing in it but roofers; all human activity was taken up with roofing, and still there were leaks.

Henrietta is sleeping late.

This is not like her. She usually gets up early. There is always work to do. Her part-time job at the museum. Letters to be written to the editor, prisoners to be visited, other people's children to be tended to.

She is on her back with her mouth open, her eyes half open, too. I touch her hand, trying to wake her without startling her, when I realize she is not sleeping at all.

I have never seen a dead person before, and I am not so much frightened as astounded.

What astounds me is that the world, including me, can keep on going without her.

Before I leave Henrietta, I bring a bucket up from the kitchen to catch the leak that is wetting the foot of her bed, which will ruin the mattress if we are not careful.

THIRTY-FOUR

Despite the downpour, Drayton Guerard arrived at The Cup by eight A.M. I was already inside. The front window of the restaurant was clouded with steam and smoke, and I saw him materialize out of the humidity like a thunderstorm, throwing off bad weather. He shook his black umbrella furiously, sending water everywhere. He stamped his feet. He reminded me of one of those burly golden retrievers people downtown keep in yards too small for them; he was too full of energy for the territory.

I apologized for coming without an appointment. "I don't have appointments," Drayton said. "I gave that up a couple of years ago. Good idea in principle, but never seemed to work. Catch as catch can."

I was breathless, but I did my best to explain the emergency.

"Henrietta is dead. The house is open. I think someone has stolen the silver, and I can't find Frank. My father is sending in the sheriff. He's probably there by now."

Drayton took a sip of his coffee. He closed his eyes and rolled the hot liquid around on his tongue, savoring it. His one remaining vice.

The eyes — older than I remembered them — opened wide now. They were eerily gray, almost colorless, and watery.

"Slow down. One problem at a time. Now, what makes you think Henrietta is dead?"

"She *is* dead. I've seen her. She is just lying there, not breathing, definitely dead. I've never seen a dead person before, but . . . but Henrietta is . . . dead."

"I see. Well, that is probably not an emergency. Nor, I think, is it even a cause for great concern. Except, of course, if it affects your legal position in this case. Henrietta, to the extent Henrietta ever acknowledged the Higher Power, has been praying for years to be delivered from these mortal chains before she became a burden."

"A burden?" I couldn't imagine Henrietta being a burden to anybody.

"Yes." Drayton took his wet coat off and hung it

over the back of the chair. "She was terrified of having to be looked after. None of her children live here anymore. She didn't want anybody to have to take care of her."

This struck me as illogical, because if there was anything Henrietta seemed to believe in, it was taking care of people. But then, she wasn't always logical.

"Now, what about the silver?" By this time he had pulled out a little pad, and was scratching notes on the damp paper.

"All that silver stuff she keeps in the dining room is gone. I don't know why I noticed it, but the door was open . . ."

"That's not an emergency. Some thief is probably on his way to Paris with the proceeds. Receiving stolen goods, a time-honored way to wealth without the risk of life imprisonment. Not an emergency. Next."

"My father is sending the sheriff after my tapes."

All of a sudden, for the first time since Hal left, I was crying. I couldn't stop. Something about *saying* it, that my own father would send the law after my private thoughts, made me feel so cold I couldn't control the huge shivers that came over me.

I was already wet all over, and Drayton was drenched, too, so when he pulled me close to his chest we both dissolved into one big damp blob, and I couldn't tell which one of us was shaking more.

My lawyer recovered first. He motioned to the waitress, who acted as if this carrying on was no big deal, just the normal sort of thing for early morning at the restaurant. She brought me a tissue and refilled Drayton's cup.

He looked at his watch. "Look, we'll have to move fast. Don't say anything about Henrietta — not to anybody. I don't want Walter Martin and Sonia Leonard to take advantage of the situation. I'll have to call Henrietta's children, but they'll cooperate. I think we can postpone the obituary a couple of days and the funeral a couple more. But still not much time." He stood up.

"Now, you need to get on to school, don't you?" I told him I really didn't feel like going to school. Gerunds and infinitives and the products of South American countries, integral numbers and things like that would be unbearable under the circumstances.

He scribbled something on the note pad, tore it off, and gave it to me.

I could barely decipher the hieroglyphics:

"Please excuse Margaret Whitford from school this morning. She has an important conference with her Guardian *ad litem* regarding the upcoming trial."

I must have looked confused.

"Keep this in case you need it later. Now go talk to Henrietta. She's waiting."

"Where?"

"Wherever you think she might feel most comfortable. Somewhere where there won't be a lot of people. A quiet place. I'm sure you'll find it."

Just as I was about to leave, he put his hand on my shoulder and said, "Remember King Solomon. Remember the baby and the sword? Well, Mac, *you're* going to be both."

THIRTY-FIVE

From The Coffee Cup it's only three blocks to Henrietta's gateway, which opens onto the path that leads to the graveyard. You pass the lawyers' offices on Broad Street, with their small, dignified black-and-gold signs swinging in the wind, city hall, the post office, the old courthouse, and then you turn (if you are on foot, or on a bicycle, as Henrietta might be), and go the wrong way up King Street past the drugstore and the antique shops.

The city is getting ready for its morning business: lawyers arriving with their briefcases, shopkeepers fumbling for their keys, a wino waiting at the locked door of the liquor store.

The first thing you will notice is how messy it is, this graveyard. Vines grow uncontrolled around the taller monuments, and the grass is coming up between the bricks on the path that winds its way around to the church. "Unitarians thrive on weeds; they like a little wildness," Henrietta has said. Next door, the Lutherans have clipped every stray stem and mowed their grass to a perfect green carpet, and it is lovely, but nothing like the magic in this place.

Here the flowers grow almost wild: Confederate roses, spiderwort, hibiscus, and honeysuckle. It's too early for the crape myrtles to bloom, but they are eery and dreamy with moss clinging to their bark. The wind rattles the palmettos.

The rain is coming down harder now. A yellow cat rubs its back against the gravestone at my feet. "Eugenia, daughter of Wm. and Ann Estill, died July 27, 1888." Nearby, a stone marked only "Our Brother, died June 10, 1886, age ten."

It is remarkable how many of these graves are children's. Abigail Bailey died in 1897 at fifteen. Many died younger. These are the graves with only a couple of feet between the headstone and the footstone. Small bodies, later joined by their parents.

Whole families lie together. James and Alice Ann Chapman, and beside them their children, Catherine Adela and James, Jr. Generations of Harbesons, some of the graves so old you can't tell who they belong to anymore.

The rain slaps my cheeks, sharp and cold. It's crazy to stay out here now, but at the same time it is the only place I can be right now, and be *me*. Any other place, with other people, their questions, their innocent conversation, would be all wrong.

I find a dry spot on a concrete bench under a large oak at the back of the graveyard. It is incredible to think that only half a block away, people are going about their business as usual — selling things, buying things, arguing in courtrooms. It is miraculous, really, the way they just keep living, unaware of this place and its secrets, unaware of Henrietta's death.

At the far corner, beside a crumbling brick wall and almost out of sight behind an explosion of tall red flowers I don't know the name of, I find him: "Dr. Augustus Ravenel Middleton, husband of Henrietta P. L. Middleton, b. 1899, d. 1980." The gravestone is twice as wide as it needs to be for just one life; Henrietta has left plenty of room for her own name and dates.

Next to the large gray stone are two small ones, obviously older. An angels stands between them, a baby angel with a pouty mouth, patiently holding her granite tablet as she has held it for all these years: "Ann and Tom, b. May 26, 1948, d. June 7, 1948."

These are Henrietta's babies, children she has never spoken of.

I talk to Henrietta, wherever she is, about her children, her life, her leaving me. We say goodbye.

I sit on the bench for a long time, until the rain stops and the sky opens like a curtain at a play, into another world.

I feel bold, as if I am on a stage, moving gracefully, effortlessly, speaking my part without hesitation.

People are clapping.

I speak my lines with confidence, my voice strong enough to hold both joy and sorrow. I tell the story of Mollie and Hal, Michael McMenamin and Mary the Rat. I laugh and I cry.

They are still clapping. When I bow, they stand up, and the sound of their shouting and clapping is deafening.

I turn back into the darkness, down the path back to the busy street, where my real life is, but I can still hear them saying, "Bravo, bravo."

THIRTY-SIX

I know you want to know how it all turned out. I'll tell you, but only if you promise not to say to yourself, "Oh yes, I knew that. I *knew* that's what would happen."

Because, of course, we all know it could have turned out some other way. As Drayton says, the Higher Power could have wanted a different ending, or she might simply have been taking the day off.

This is what happened, according to Drayton Guerard.

Right after he left The Cup that morning, and while I sat in the rain with Henrietta's husband and her dead babies, Drayton Guerard called a meeting with Walter Martin, Sonia Leonard, and their clients.

It was urgent, he said. The Whitford child is in bad shape. She's furious that anybody's even *talking* about making her tapes an exhibit in some case file. She's adamant that her therapist may not testify about any of their conversations. If Judge Judge makes Harvey testify, Mac says, she will insist on testifying herself and she will say everything she has wanted to say all these months.

He met with my father first.

"It's not good," said Drayton to Hal, while Walter Martin pushed nervously at his cuticles. "If you insist on having the court listen to the tapes, your daughter will play them for the Judge herself. And she'll read the diary. She's a very good reader, don't you think, quite dramatic? There's a lot of stuff in there I don't think you'll want to hear."

Walter Leonard finally managed to interrupt: "Are you threatening my client, Guerard? Because if you are . . ."

"I certainly am," said my lawyer, "and I think he has enough sense to realize that the real threat is in those tapes, not in anything this old curmudgeon has to say."

Drayton left my father and his lawyer and went several doors down Broad Street to Sonia Leonard's office, where Sonia and Mollie were waiting.

To Mollie (as Sonia Leonard sat with her mouth

shut for the first time Drayton could ever remember) he said, "It's not a pretty picture. If you insist on fighting for custody, your husband will try to introduce Mac's diary and her tapes into evidence. I'm going to object to it, but the older I get the more energy it takes for me to jump up and make objections, and the less they seem to matter. You may lose custody, but worse, whatever relationship you have with Mac will be ruined. And let me remind you, if I may, madam, about your testimony at the deposition, during which you made numerous suggestions about how you might redo your own daughter."

Drayton made these speeches without having the slightest idea where my diary was, or the tapes. It was weeks later before Frank, the ex-con, got up the nerve to take them to Drayton's office, along with the three pillowcases of silver he had removed from Henrietta's house. When he'd gone up to take her some coffee and discovered her dead, his first instinct was to call an ambulance, or the police, but his only involvement with blue lights and sirens had been so unpleasant that he couldn't bring himself to do this, so he packed the valuable stuff the best he could, fearing someone *else* might take it. He knew how she loved to keep the silver shining, how she wouldn't save it just for holidays, because, as she said, "Every day is a holiday, Frank, if we want to celebrate."

Mollie and Hal settled their case. Not forever, but for the time being. *I* get the house. My own bedroom all the time, no back and forth.

Mollie and Hal move back and forth. They share Hal's apartment, Mollie one week, Hal the next. Mollie has redone the place. With his permission, she's thrown out most of the funky stuff he bought at the flea market and created an "environment" that she says suits him better. She hasn't managed to renovate Hal yet, but I think she's finally given up on that.

Hal has dumped Mary the Rat, which is good, because I doubt if Mary Rattick would have fit into Mollie's décor.

Michael McMenamin still comes around occasionally, but the last time he came he got his weeks mixed up, and ended up bringing roses to Hal, who wasn't at all happy to be waked up at six in the morning.

Drayton cautions me not to get too comfortable. The house will have to be sold. I have my home back now because my parents couldn't bring themselves to hear what I really had to say about them. They won't be expected to share an apartment forever now that they're divorced, even if they're never there together.

"This is not a permanent arrangement, kid," Drayton says, squeezing my hand. "The house will take a while to sell at the price your parents have put on it, but sooner or later you're going to have to move. I think you can handle it. And you know where to find me if you need any help."

THIRTY-SEVEN

Things have settled down now. It's summer, and too hot for arguments. People run from their air-conditioned houses to their air-conditioned cars and into their air-conditioned offices, and for most of them it's enough of a goal in life just to stay cool.

I like the drama of the weather this time of year. The days begin damp and balmy, work themselves up into a fever by noon, and by late afternoon burst into thunderstorms that sweep across the city like serious temper tantrums.

I like to sit in a rocking chair on the upstairs porch and watch the black clouds build up in the western sky over the Ashley River, watch them coming closer and closer until they capture my street. I like the moment before the rain comes, when the air smells dark and electric and evil. And then the explosion of thunder and rain, the bad temper finally letting go, and the relief that follows.

This is the best time to take a nap, when the rain beats in a steady rhythm against the tin roof.

I gave up naps in kindergarten because I didn't like the idea of enforced sleep. I remember lying on my plastic mat at the Montessori school, determined to keep my eyes open while the other kids snored and sucked their thumbs. I had a strip of blanket lining, slick and satiny, the remains of a beat-up baby blanket, and Mollie would pack it in my lunch box every day. It was the last piece of my babyhood; for years I had fingered it to put myself to sleep. On the day I decided to give up naps I threw the piece of lining away and from then on I stayed awake.

But I have come back to taking naps. I don't know what it is, but I feel exhausted all the time. Part of it is physical. I'm growing taller — an inch in the last three months — and I've gone up two shoe sizes in a year. But it's more than that. I have so many decisions to make: what courses to take next fall, whether I'll try out for the debating team (I'll be going to the public high school, which disappoints Mollie, but she and Hal let me choose). Sometimes all these decisions weigh down on me so much that all I want to do is crawl into bed and pull a pillow over my head.

This particular afternoon, with the rain drumming the roof and the thunder far enough away for comfort, I dream of Henrietta's house. Like most dreams, it is nonsense, but the nonsense has a certain ring of truth.

Henrietta is having a tea party on her side porch. Drayton Guerard is there, spilling tea on his necktie and being nice to Walter Martin and Sonia Leonard, who are playing croquet together in Henrietta's yard, which is blossoming with all sorts of impossible flowers — giant flowers as tall as people, in neon colors.

Mollie and Hal are there, not speaking. They have joined some new religious group, wear bright orange robes, and have taken a vow of silence. And Michael McMenamin and Mary the Rat are at the far end of the porch, on an old settee, kissing and laughing.

Frank, the ex-con, gets out of a big blue Mercedes and comes up the steps to the porch carrying a briefcase full of silver — forks and knives in old-fashioned fancy patterns, which he presents to Henrietta with great ceremony, and after she kisses him on the cheek she asks him how his course in Receiving Stolen Goods is going. She turns to her guests and explains that Frank is a full professor now, and his classes at the college are overflowing.

Of course, none of this ever happened. And when I wake up I remember where I really am, and what has really happened in my world. That, too, is strange, but in a more predictable way.

Henrietta left her house to the city, with only one catch: they have to use it as a halfway house for ex-cons. Drayton Guerard is the trustee. He's doing fine, even though he's getting older and sloppier and poorer, because now, in addition to all the Alcoholics Anonymous he represents for free, he has kids from all over the county calling for the best lawyer in Charleston. Word got around that he could get a kid out of bad situation pretty fast. No, they always say, there's no money in it, but it's a really interesting story. And of course, Drayton never could resist an interesting story.

Harvey is an expectant mother. About a month after my case settled she started corresponding with an orphanage in Argentina, and in a couple of weeks she'll be flying down to pick up her kid, a three-year-old girl with black sparkling eyes and curly hair. She'll have to cut back to part-time, but that's okay, she says, because she's going to have plenty to do now that she has somebody to cook for. I won't be

coming for therapy anymore, I tell her, but she's going to need a babysitter.

Hal and Mollie are doing okay. Hal has decided
he likes being a lawyer after all, or at least he'd
better like it, because money is tight. My parents
gave Walter Martin and Sonia Leonard most of what
had been set aside for my college education, and
since I've got my heart set on New York University
and an apartment in Washington Square, Hal and
Mollie are going to have to start saving again in
earnest. It's a good thing Mollie's business is
expanding. She flies off to places like India and
Thailand to consult with big corporations about how
to "do over" their new executives.

The every-other-week arrangement has fallen by
the wayside because of Mollie's schedule. She's not
uptight about giving up "her week" anymore, and
even though Hal says he's "thrilled" to have more
time with me, I can tell he's getting a little
exhausted by all this extra responsibility.

One part of the dream really did come true.
Michael McMenamin and Mary Rattick are dating.
I think they are just perfect for each other.

My house has been for sale for a couple of
months now. Mollie and Hal are asking a fortune for
it, but still people come almost every day to look. I'm

getting to know all the real estate agents by their first names, and they are beginning to realize that there's not a chance the house will sell until I'm back in school. I entertain myself pointing out defects to potential buyers. "It's a great old place," I'll say, "if you're into restoration." I remember what Henrietta said about her place: "It's a regular maintenance nightmare."

I know I'll be moving, but for now I have my own house, in my own neighborhood, in this city I love.

The phone rings and I run for it.

"Mac? It's Evelyn. Listen, Tim's back. Yeah. Just for a visit. He asked about you, and I thought maybe I'd have a party. Well, not really a party — just the four of us. What do you think?"

I tell her I think it'll be great. "I have a lot to tell you guys," I say, "A lot of stuff has happened."

I hang up the phone. I rub the sleep from my eyes and wipe the fog from the window that looks out over my backyard. Mollie's flower beds are over-grown now, but I like it better this way. The sun is setting, sending its fiery colors across the treetops. In minutes the spectacle is gone, and the whole town seems satisfied with just *being*.

Then I see the blue hydrangea. It must have blossomed overnight, or maybe I've just been too busy to notice.